T0301192

ANGÉLIQUE

Guillaume Musso is the no. 1 bestselling author in France. He is the author of *The Reunion*, *The Secret Life of Writers* and *The Stranger in the Seine*, among others. His novels have been translated into 47 languages and have sold 34 million copies worldwide. He was born in Antibes, in the South of France, and currently lives in Paris.

Also by Guillaume Musso

THE STRANGER IN THE SEINE

THE SECRET LIFE OF WRITERS

THE REUNION

ANGÉLIQUE

A NOVEL

GUILLAUME MUSSO

TRANSLATED FROM THE FRENCH
BY ROSIE EYRE

WEIDENFELD & NICOLSON

First published in Great Britain in 2024
by Weidenfeld & Nicolson
an imprint of The Orion Publishing Group Ltd
Carmelite House, 50 Victoria Embankment
London EC4Y 0DZ

An Hachette UK Company

e authorised representative in the EEA is Hachette Ireland,
8 Castlecourt Centre, Dublin 15, D15 XTP3, Ireland (email: info@hbgi.ie)

First published in French as *Angélique* by Calmann-Lévy.

3 5 7 9 10 8 6 4 2

A CIP catalogue record for this book is
available from the British Library.

ISBN (Hardback) 9781399615570
ISBN (Export Trade Paperback) 9781399626675
ISBN (eBook) 9781399615600
ISBN (Audio) 9781399615617

Typeset by Input Data Services Ltd, Bridgwater, Somerset

Printed in Great Britain by Clays Ltd, Elcograf, S.p.A.

www.orionbooks.co.uk
www.weidenfeldandnicolson.co.uk

For Ingrid, Nathan and Flora

I

LOUISE COLLANGE

1

THE GIRL WITH THE CELLO

1

Paris
Pompidou Hospital
Monday, 27 December

A shaft of light in a storm-tossed sky. That was the image the music conjured in his mind. The cello's long phrase rose and fell hypnotically, like an invitation to surrender. In his semi-conscious state, Mathias felt his breathing melt to the rhythm of the melody. Carried by the notes, he retreated into himself with a calm he hadn't known in a long time. Sensations flashed back to the surface. The blue of the Mediterranean, bodies lazing on the sand, kisses on salty lips.

But his joy was fragile. A storm was brewing nearby, dissonant feelings entwining in a fraught mash-up of frivolity and calamity. Suddenly the harmony was shattered, as if the bow had screeched off its strings, dashing all promises of pleasure.

Mathias Taillefer opened his eyes.

He was lying on a hospital bed, dressed in one of those

hideous, washed-out cotton gowns that put the buttocks at the mercy of every passing draught. Two tubes snaked from the catheter that had been planted in his arm, while a cardiac monitor to his left traced the feverish beating of his heart. In the next bed, his geriatric roommate hadn't stirred all day, giving him the nasty impression of having been admitted to intensive care rather than a cardiology ward. The mournful patter of rain had replaced the warm thrum of the cello, and instead of the Mediterranean, the murky Paris skies cast everything in grim shades of grey. For a moment, the music in his dream had transported him away from the hospital, but the respite had been short-lived.

Life was a bitch.

With some effort, Mathias rearranged his pillow to prop himself up. And that was when he saw her, half-steeped in shadow: the outline of a young woman, sitting ramrod straight on a chair, with a cello angled between her legs. So, the music hadn't just been in his head.

'Who are you?' he grunted.

'My name's Louise. Louise Collange.'

From her girlish voice, she couldn't be more than a teenager, but she didn't seem remotely intimidated.

'And what the . . . and what are you doing in my room, Louise Collange? You think this is the place to be practising for your school concert?'

'I'm a volunteer for a charity called Musicians in Hospitals,' she replied.

As she moved closer, Mathias narrowed his eyes for a better view of her. Oval face framed by sheets of blonde hair, dimpled chin, Peter Pan collar jumper, flared velvet skirt, leather ankle boots. A beacon of light in the gloom of the hospital.

4

'Didn't you like it?'

'What, your scrap of Schubert? No, it set my teeth on edge . . . and my head on fire.'

'That's a bit strong.'

'. . . *And* it woke me up.'

Louise shrugged, visibly miffed.

'People normally enjoy it.'

'They enjoy someone hassling them in their sickbed?'

'It's called counter-stimulation,' the girl explained, dragging over the red faux-leather chair to perch next to him. 'The music fires up alternative sensory pathways that distract the patient from the pain.'

'What a load of crap,' he huffed, shaking his head. 'Fancy yourself as a doctor, do you? Where did you read that?'

'In a medical textbook, as it happens. I'm a second-year med student.'

'But how old are you?'

'Seventeen. I skipped two years.'

If she thought that would impress him . . . Taillefer remained stubbornly unmoved. In the chrome-plated bed rails, he glimpsed flickers of his haggard reflection: wild hair, greying temples, a week's worth of stubble, dark-blue eyes dulled by exhaustion.

'Right, Louise,' he continued. 'If you've finished your little recital, you can leave us in peace now.'

He nodded at the neighbouring bed. 'I don't think your music stands a hope of reviving Colonel Sanders here.'

'Your call.'

As the young woman replaced the cello in its case, Taillefer rubbed his eyes wearily. He'd been admitted the previous day after a seemingly mild heart attack, but had still required

5

a raft of tests, given his history as a transplant patient. If the results passed muster, he might have a chance of being discharged the following day. In the meantime, he was stuck in that grim room, waiting out the hours in its haze of looming death.

He couldn't stop thinking about his dog, alone in the house, and about the dire weather that had been lashing Paris as the year petered to an end: weeks of torrential rain and heavy skies, a horizon that had been clogged for so long, it was impossible to imagine spring ever returning. And now, this girl who wouldn't leave . . .

'Are you still here?' he snapped.

'Two minutes! I'm putting my sheets away.'

'Don't you have better things to do than going around hospitals, acting like you're Jacqueline du Pré?'

Louise shrugged again.

'Who's Jacqueline du Pré?'

'Look her up later. Seriously, get out of this hellhole and do what people your age should be doing.'

'And what should "people my age" be doing?'

'I dunno, going out with your girlfriends, hanging around with boys, getting off your face . . .'

'Very inspiring.'

His tone hardened. 'That's enough. Scram, get lost. Go home, if you don't have any friends.'

'You really are a charmer.'

'You're the one coming in here giving me earache!' he retorted.

A long gurgle rippled from his gut. He patted his stomach with a grimace.

'And I'm starving. Actually, if you want to make yourself

useful, you can find me something to eat before you go.'

'I'll ask the nurses.'

'No, for pity's sake! I don't want their godforsaken mush. There's a café in the lobby – Relais H. Grab me a ham baguette with butter or a smoked salmon roll.'

'Sure you don't want a beer while I'm there? Salt isn't good for the heart, you know.'

'Just do what I'm asking, please. It'll cheer me up more than your Schubert.'

Louise paused for a second.

'Will you watch my cello?'

He nodded.

'Don't worry.'

2

Once he and Colonel Sanders were alone again, Taillefer checked his watch. It wasn't yet 4 p.m. and already it was nearly dark. He raised his hand to the scar that sliced his thorax in two. For five and a half years now, he'd been living with someone else's heart. Over time, as the mark had faded, so had his fear grown that one day the replacement would give up on him. He closed his eyes. The previous day, by the beehives in Parc Montsouris, he'd truly believed his hour had come. He'd been hit by a searing feeling in his chest, then the sensation of a vice crushing his heart. The pain had spread as far as his jaw, causing him to stumble, gagging and gasping for breath, as if he'd just run a cross-country race.

He'd only regained consciousness in the ambulance, on the way to Pompidou Hospital. While the initial tests had been reassuring, his fear refused to leave him. The hospital terrified him. Its sinister atmosphere, the rank food, the infantilisation of the patients, the plastic bottle you were forced to piss into, the high risk of catching an infection while you were there. He couldn't shake the visceral conviction that you might come in for a scratch and be carted out feet first.

'Grub's up!'

Taillefer jolted to attention. Louise Collange was waving a paper bag in front of her.

'I got you this,' she announced, pulling out a salad box. 'It'll do you more good.'

'Are you having a laugh?' he blurted. 'Why the fuck did you do that? I asked for a salmon or . . .'

'Relax, the salad's for me. Here's your sandwich!'

He glowered back at her – *not* the kind of joke he found funny – and unwrapped his roll while muttering darkly.

'Don't feel obliged to keep me company,' he told her as she reoccupied her seat next to him. 'Really, don't.'

'Is it true you're a cop?'

He scowled. It was going to be a long day.

'Who told you that?'

'I heard the nurses talking. They were saying you work for the Major Crime Unit.'

Taillefer shook his head.

'That was in another life. I quit the police five years ago.'

'How old are you?'

'Forty-seven.'

'That's young to retire.'

'That's life,' he replied, biting off a hunk of bread.

'What happened?' she pressed. 'Was it because of your heart problems?'

'That's absolutely none of your business.'

'And what are you doing now?'

'I'm listening to you giving me the third degree,' he sighed, 'and wondering what the hell I've done to deserve it.'

'You're a tough customer, aren't you?'

'Well spotted.'

He finished his sandwich in silence, then took a firmer tack.

'Listen, Louise, you're obviously a very exceptional young woman, but I don't like people bothering me. I'm sure there are patients down the corridor who'll love your do-gooding. But I couldn't give a flying fuck about your life, your feelings or anything you might care to tell me about. And contrary to appearances, I'm not a nice guy. So I'm going to ask you politely, one last time, to leave me in peace. Otherwise—'

'Otherwise what?' she interrupted. 'You'll call for a nurse?'

'Otherwise, I'll get up and kick you out of here myself,' he replied calmly. 'Arse first. Is that clear?'

'If you're at a loose end, I might have a job for you.'

'I'm not looking for a job!' he shouted. 'I'm trying to get some rest!'

'I could pay you. I have money, you know.'

Amazed by her gall, Taillefer faltered for a moment. With her infuriating persistence, she reminded him of a female François Pignon – a slapstick comedy-style nuisance that he was *seriously* going to need military force to see off.

'I'd like you to investigate my mum's death.'

'I thought I said . . .'

'She died three months ago.'

'I'm sorry for your loss.'

Louise nodded, and Taillefer felt duty-bound to continue.

9

'How did she die?'

'In an accident, according to the police.'

'And according to you?'

'I think she was murdered.'

At that moment, a nurse swung open the door to do her rounds. She checked the drips, the vital signs on the monitor and the saturation levels on the oximeter, while making limp attempts at conversation. Taillefer toyed with asking if she could give the girl her marching orders while she was there, but ultimately kept silent. As soon as she was gone, Louise picked up from where she'd left off.

'I'd like you to have a look at the case, make a few calls, maybe—'

'What case?'

'Start by reading the press coverage of her death. Type her name into a search engine.'

'No way.'

'It'll take a couple of hours of your time. And you can ask me for anything in return.'

There was a spirited glint in the young woman's eyes. A brilliant and troubling light.

'Yeah, right. Seriously?'

Suddenly a thought occurred to him, one which could at least relieve part of the anxiety that had been nagging him since he'd arrived at the hospital.

'Will you go and feed my dog? I left him back home.'

'And in return you'll pick up the investigation about my mum?'

'No, no! In return, I'll spend a couple of hours reading news articles about your mum's death. Not the same thing.'

'Done. What kind of dog is he?'

'A German shepherd. He's called Titus.'

'Is he friendly?'

'Not in the slightest. And he doesn't like nuisances either, so watch yourself.'

Taillefer gave Louise his keys, the alarm code and his address in Square de Montsouris.

'Here's the deal: you go in, you feed Titus and you come straight back out again, without touching anything in the house. Understood?'

'Understood,' she agreed. 'How will we catch up afterwards?'

'Leave me your number. I'll call you. What was your mum's name?'

'Petrenko. The prima ballerina, Stella Petrenko.'

2

THE FALL OF STELLA PETRENKO

1

7 p.m.

Lying back on his hospital bed, Mathias Taillefer connected his laptop to his phone. The signal wasn't great, but it was better than nothing. From his headphones came the familiar strum of Pat Metheny's guitar. Through the window, the desolate, rain-lashed darkness of the Parisian night. Taillefer tapped away on his keyboard in search of information about Louise's mother. Although Stella Petrenko's name rang a bell, he was incapable of putting a face to her. And the news of her death had completely passed him by.

He downloaded a selection of articles from the main national newspapers, then studied them in chronological order until a fairly complete portrait of the ballerina emerged.

Standing at five foot seven, with her beanpole legs and swan-like neck, Stella Petrenko had been one of the stars of the French classical dance scene of the 1990s and 2000s. Born in Marseille in 1969, to an unassuming family originating from the Ukrainian city of Lviv, she'd moved to the capital at the age of twelve to join the Paris Opera Ballet School. As an archetypal product of the Palais Garnier system, she'd climbed the ranks with steely determination. At seventeen, she'd progressed to the main company and had continued her rise over the years that followed – first as a junior *quadrille*, then as a *coryphée* and a *sujet*, before landing the dual lead role of Odette and Odile in *Swan Lake* at the age of twenty-two. But that same year, she'd been hit by a motorbike in central Paris. The accident had left her needing surgery, followed by a long spell of rehabilitation, putting her career on hold. For the rest of her life, Stella was plagued by back and knee troubles. Yet despite that blow from fate, she'd fought her way back to the top and, through sheer perseverance, pulled off a return to the stage. She'd finally reached the hallowed status of prima ballerina relatively late, at the age of thirty.

Petrenko had worked with the leading choreographers of the day – the likes of Maurice Béjart, William Forsythe and Pina Bausch – and had delivered some memorable perform-ances in the *Rite of Spring* and Ravel's *Boléro*. She'd netted roles in highbrow ad campaigns for Repetto, Hermès and AcquaAlta, but successive injuries had marred the final years of her career: always her back, and the ligaments in her bad knee. On turning forty-two, the mandatory retirement age for Paris Opera ballerinas, she'd ruefully hung up her pumps.

Her daughter was born in 2004, conceived with her then-partner Laurent Collange, first violinist with the Radio France Philharmonic Orchestra.

Taillefer unplugged his headphones and cracked open a can of Coke Zero, which an unscrupulous nursing assistant had procured for him in exchange for a ten-euro note. On YouTube, he loaded a clip from Prokofiev's *Romeo and Juliet*, in which Stella had danced the lead. The footage disturbed him.

Stella Petrenko was a far cry from the lithe, doll-faced stereotype of the ballerinas who featured each year in the Épinal ice championships. At first sight, her appearance lacked any real grace, her features bearing no obvious mark of her Ukrainian roots. Ripped torso, overlong legs sculpted by eight hours a day of training, skeletal-looking arms. There was the same jarring, severe quality about her face. Sunken cheeks, disproportionately large, haunted eyes, jet-black hair that kept escaping in rogue wisps from her taut bun.

But as soon as she started moving, the magic clicked into place. Through a strange alchemy, onstage Petrenko was a picture of grace and femininity. This peculiar ability, the transfixing aura she conjured from nowhere, unsettled Taillefer even through the screen. Like the angel's share of an aged Armagnac.

The cop rounded off his search with a slideshow on an opera website that retraced the dancer's career. Over the course of his reading he'd learnt a lot, and, without ever having met her, he felt a tug of sympathy for Louise's mother. As he scrolled through the pictures, he could imagine how tough her path had been. A gifted, solitary child who'd given her heart and soul to dance. An adolescence spent in a brutally competitive world where only the strongest survived. A life of struggle and sacrifice that had been shot down in its ascendency by a twist of fate, followed by a fresh fight to claw herself back into the light. A gruelling life driven by the intoxicating adrenaline of the stage. A lurching, fitful life

14

of highs and lows, which must have left her with a sense of unfinished business. Little known by the wider public, Stella Petrenko might have secured the crown of prima ballerina, but only at the eleventh hour, and even then, on the big day itself – the day that should have been the most wonderful of her life, the culmination of thousands of hours of work – fate had again intervened, this time in the form of a strike by the Opera's casual staff, which had forced the company to perform the show without costumes or props.

In an interview with a Sunday magazine to mark her swansong, Stella had spoken excitedly about all her plans for the next stage of her career – cinema, theatre, fashion . . . Ten years on, very few of them had come to pass. The dancer had vanished into the media wilderness, not to be spoken of again until the announcement of her death.

2

Taillefer drained his Coke and rubbed his screen-weary eyes, before slipping on his reading glasses to resume his search.

Stella Petrenko's death, reported at the end of the previous summer, hadn't made the front pages. It had barely warranted a catch-all tweet from the French minister of culture: *It is with great sadness that I learn of the sudden passing of Stella Petrenko, one of the most celebrated prima ballerinas of recent decades. A devotee of her art and a defender of her freedoms as a woman, she embodied these values in her skilful and sensitive performances.*

Admittedly, the dancer hadn't chosen the best moment to bow out. On 6 September 2021, the world had also learnt of the death of Jean-Paul Belmondo. *Unlucky to the last,*

Taillefer thought with a grimace. He remembered a radio programme he'd heard once, in which Jean D'Ormesson had mused entertainingly on the perils of dying on the same day as a celebrity more famous than yourself. The writer had cited the examples of Jean Cocteau, whose passing had been eclipsed by that of Edith Piaf, and the late Aldous Huxley, who'd died on the day of JFK's assassination. Then there was Farrah Fawcett, the *Charlie's Angels* star Taillefer had been besotted with as a twelve-year-old. She'd had the misfortune to die on the same day as Michael Jackson.

In short, the departure of the Man from Acapulco had erased the dancer's demise from the TV news tribute slots and newspaper culture pages. It had taken until late afternoon the following day for the French news agency AFP to announce her death, in a dispatch that was hardly picked up on the websites of the main media outlets.

Stella Petrenko dies in fall from fifth floor
AFP

The former Paris Opera prima ballerina suffered a fatal fall from the balcony of her flat in Rue de Bellechasse. She was fifty-two years old.

The incident took place at around 11.30 p.m. yesterday evening, from the fifth-floor balcony of the six-storey building at 31, Rue de Bellechasse in the 7th arrondissement.

Emergency services arrived on the scene shortly afterwards, after neighbours raised the alarm. Ms Petrenko was still alive when the ambulance team arrived, but had sustained serious head injuries and damage to her upper and lower limbs. Despite their efforts to revive her, she was pronounced dead twenty minutes later.

The circumstances surrounding the incident remain unclear. *'Accidental fall or attempted suicide? We'll need to wait for the findings of the investigation,'* a Paris Judicial Police source commented, stressing that any criminal involvement had been ruled out. The public prosecutor's office signalled that an autopsy was underway to determine the exact cause of death. [. . .]

Taillefer reread the article to make sure nothing had escaped him. The press agency's account raised more questions than answers. If he wanted to know more, he'd have to call in a favour from his former colleagues.

But who could he turn to, after hours on 27 December? He scratched his chin, racking his brains. Who'd taken up the case? Not his old unit in Major Crime, based on the details in the article. It must have been entrusted to the Left Bank branch of the Judicial Police. The last he'd heard, the crew was being headed up by Serge Cabrera. The JP skipper's image flashed into his mind: strapping frame, bull neck, shirt buttons always on the brink of bursting, mullet straight from the 1980s. Known as 'the Niçoise' after his home city, Cabrera was notorious for his boorishness, sexism and potty mouth, which had fallen increasingly adrift of the times. Perhaps he wasn't even in post anymore, forced out by #MeToo or some other blunder. After checking he still had his number, Taillefer composed a text to put out some feelers. He didn't have high hopes. Between Christmas and New Year, nobody would be rushing to help him.

What now?

Returning to his laptop, he dimmed his bed light and launched a video of Maurice Béjart's choreography of Ravel's *Boléro*, one of the routines that had made Stella Petrenko's name.

3

14th arrondissement

In the drizzle, the unlicensed voiturette had the look of a yogurt pot. A caramel-flavoured Danette trundling along in the mass of the traffic. At the wheel, Louise regretted having taken the logjammed boulevards that skirted the edges of the city. She rammed on the accelerator, but the motor, capped at twenty-eight miles per hour, was already going flat out. Laid beside her on the plastic seat, her cello swallowed up the space. Coupled with the damp air leaching into the passenger compartment, it made her feel suddenly claustrophobic. She sneezed. To eke out the battery, she'd resisted turning on the heating, but her teeth were chattering.

She left the boulevards at Portes de Vanves to weave through the motley streets of Petit-Montrouge. Night was falling, swathing the city in icy gloom, while sheets of fog swirled at the feet of buildings – a rare sight in Paris.

While she waited at the lights, Louise entered the address Tailler had given her, then propped her phone against the windscreen and let the GPS guide her. She continued past Place Denfert-Rochereau, where the square's iconic lion loomed as if frozen in the middle of a ghostly savannah, then on towards Cité Universitaire. As she neared the campus, she recognised the grassy fortress of the Montsouris reservoir, which supplied a large portion of the capital's drinking water. Until now she'd been in charted territory, but the sense of familiarity vanished as the route steered her onto Square de Montsouris.

The Danette was forced to slow as it rolled up the narrow cobbles. The little private street was incongruous, but it exuded a rustic charm. Despite the darkness, ivy- and wisteria-covered façades could be seen peeping from behind the rows of wrought-iron railings. Handsome detached art deco houses interspersed with artists' studios drenched in greenery.

Louise parked up in front of the address Taillefer had given her. Affixed to the gate was a bright-red sign that warned, 'No Entry – Dangerous Dog', blazoned with the image of a German shepherd. She cautiously unlocked the front gates and prised one of them open. No sign of a dog in the garden. Her movements had activated the outdoor-light sensors, bringing the building into view. It looked like a country manor that had been transplanted to the middle of Paris: half-timbering, corbels, warm yellow paintwork. Taking her courage in both hands, Louise opened the front door. Immediately she was met by the shriek of the house alarm. As she punched in the code to disable the system, she barely had time to see hurtling towards her . . . an adorable, floppy-eared bundle of tawny-and-white fur. *False alarm.*

Taillefer had well and truly stitched her up. Instead of a German shepherd, she was staring down the nose of a fifteen-inch beagle.

'Hello, Titus,' she said, ruffling his ears.

Relieved to be free, the animal tore outside and ran several laps of the garden. Louise ventured further into the house. The place was nothing like how she'd pictured it. She'd imagined rocking up in a ramshackle oddball's lair. A copper's hovel smelling of sweat and tobacco, with unwashed dishes festering in the sink. She couldn't have been more wrong. By the looks of it, the house had been newly renovated, with as many walls as possible knocked through to open up the space. The décor was understated: bare wood, pale oiled parquet, Jieldé lamps in assorted sizes, an angular Barcelona Chair. Every element worked in harmony to create a flawless continuum of creamy hues. Titus had joined her in the living area and was yapping at her heels. Louise let him show her to the kitchen, where she found a shelf piled with dog food. She emptied a tin of meatballs onto a plate and refilled the water bowl, then headed back to the lounge.

Since leaving the hospital, Louise had felt exhaustion overwhelming her. She couldn't get warm, as if she were sickening for something. In the fireplace, someone had arranged a ball of newspaper, some kindling and three thick logs in a teepee formation. The temptation was too much. She struck a long match and lit the paper. As the flames began to catch, ignoring her promise to Taillefer, she set about exploring the room. Judging by the extensive bookcase, the cop was big on foreign literature, art and philosophy. From the walls hung large Chinese calligraphy prints and a Fabienne Verdier lithograph, while on the coffee table sat a bronze Bernar Venet sculpture of two entangled, deconstructed spirals. Perched on a block of petrified wood, a second sculpture depicted a figure made from a mesh of white letters: a kind of Alphabet Man in a lace suit who seemed to be keeping watch over the space.

Everything was immaculate and tastefully arranged, nothing left to chance. Whoever did the housework must have been obsessively tidy. That also explained why Louise had immediately felt at home. Disorder had always distressed her. She craved precision and symmetry. She liked things to be in their place. It struck her that there were no photos or other signs of a wife or children in Taillefer's life. She didn't dare to check upstairs. She wouldn't put it past the cop to have installed security cameras.

The young woman remained standing by the fire until her skin burned, relishing the sensation that she herself was being consumed by the flames.

Then, rubbing her eyes, she lay down for a moment on the couch – a daybed style that reminded her of one she'd seen in a psychiatrist's office. Titus came to join her, curling up against her legs. Taking out her phone, she typed Taillefer's name into the browser. He seemed to have appeared in the press twice: once in the early 2000s, in relation to a scuffle at the Gare du Nord that had turned nasty, and again in the summer of 2016, in a local paper from the south-east that had run a special feature on organ donation. Apart from those two mentions, there wasn't a scrap of information about the cop. As her eyes flickered shut, Louise asked herself who Mathias Taillefer really was. Why had she chosen to confide in him, despite his frosty demeanour and short temper? Was it honestly a good idea to have told him about her mother? But who else could she turn to? She rarely saw her father, now she had her student room in Maubert. And in any case, Laurent Collange had moved on from Stella Petrenko years earlier, without a backward glance.

4

A spiral. A vortex. A whirlwind of notes reverberating on a loop through his mind. Once more, it was music that wrenched Taillefer from sleep. But this time, the blare of his ringtone replaced Louise Collange's cello.

Unknown number. He swallowed hard and sat up in the darkness. It was past midnight. He'd drifted off in front of the images of Stella dancing Ravel's *Boléro.* His throat was dry, his aching neck making him heavy-headed. And he was desperate for a piss.

'Hello?' he asked into the receiver.

'Captain Taillefer?' a woman's voice replied.

'That's me. At least, it was.'

'Good evening. This is Lieutenant Fatoumata Diop from the Left Bank Judicial Police. Superintendent Cabrera asked me to get in touch.'

Taillefer flicked on his bedside light, pleasantly surprised by the call. Against all odds, the Niçoise had deigned to put one of his minions on the case – and quickly too.

'Thanks for phoning. As I told Cabrera, I'm after some details about the death of Stella Petrenko.'

'What kind of details?'

'Was it your unit that attended the scene?'

'Yes, we arrived just after the ambulance. If you want something specific, now's your chance. I've got the report up on the screen.'

'Any chance of sending it over? Just to save time.'

Diop exhaled deeply.

'Dream on. Listen, I'm not interested in playing games, so if—'

'What caused Stella Petrenko's death, in your opinion?' Taillefer asked, hurriedly steering the conversation back on course.

'An accident, in all probability. Or suicide, but that seems less likely.'

'And going with the accident theory, how did it happen?'

'Looks like she'd climbed a stepladder to water the planters on her balcony. We found a watering can on the pavement near the body.'

'I read that the fall happened just before midnight.'

'That's right. And?'

'Do you water your plants at midnight?'

'There's a first time for everything. It was early September, still hot and summery. The sun sets late in Paris at that time of year. People stay outside longer.'

'Yeah . . .'

'I saw the balustrade,' Diop added. 'It was rusty as hell and not very high. The balcony wouldn't have passed current regulations. A kid could easily have fallen over the edge. The woman went up a ladder to water her flowers. She'd been drinking, and she slipped. Simple as that. Game over.'

Mathias rubbed his neck.

'And the post-mortem? What did that show?'

'Not much – although she did have a gram of alcohol in her blood. She'd opened a bottle of Burgundy and downed three quarters of it that evening. And she'd been on the ganja, by the looks of it.'

'No signs of a struggle?'

'Nope.'

'Nothing on her fingernails? No traces of skin or fibres?'

'Not a sausage.'

'And that was enough to rule out any criminal involvement?'

'A crime implies a motive,' Diop replied exasperatedly. 'And we didn't find anything to suggest that was the case.'

'Nothing had been stolen from the flat?'

'There was valuable jewellery in plain sight and a substantial amount of cash in her purse. Nobody had touched them.'

'What about the suicide theory?'

'I can't really see it myself, but we did consider the possibility. She hadn't been in great shape since leaving the spotlight. Often, in the evening, she'd get dressed up as if she was going on stage again – tutu, leotard, tights, the whole shebang.'

'Had she done that on the evening she died?'

'Yes, that's how we found her. Like a dead swan that had been washed up on the pavement.'

Taillefer shuddered at the image. He was surprised a detail like that hadn't made it into the press.

'What about the weed? Did she have a lot of it on her?'

'She was growing it herself!'

'Was she dealing?'

'No, just a few plants for personal use. Anyway, Taillefer, I'd really like to get home, so—'

'Wait, you said the paramedics were the first on the scene, and from what I read, Petrenko didn't die instantly.'

'Yeah, and . . . ?'

'She didn't have chance to say anything to them?'

'What, and write "OMAR KILLED ME" in her own blood on the floor? No, she didn't have chance, because she

24

was already fit to be spooned off the pavement. You get the picture?'

'One last thing: you're certain nobody could have broken into the flat?'

'How could they? The door was locked from inside.'

Taillefer opened his mouth to continue his fact-checking, but he'd exhausted all avenues.

Before she hung up, Fatoumata Diop stuck a final nail in the coffin.

'Listen, I'd have liked to investigate the murder theory too. But trust me: we looked everywhere, we checked out everything, and we found nothing. Stella Petrenko wasn't assassinated.'

3

AN IMPOSSIBLE INVESTIGATION

1

28 December

'Wake up! Oi, wake up!'

When Louise opened her eyes, she was hit by bright daylight. A beagle was licking her face while Taillefer's enormous hand rattled her shoulder. She felt like she'd just emerged from a long tunnel, as if she'd been unconscious for days. Why had she slept for so long, and so deeply? Pent-up exhaustion from her course, the winter blues, the aftershock from her mother's death?

'Ow! Stop it! You're going to dislocate my shoulder!'

The ex-cop glowered menacingly, his whole body rigid with rage.

'What the hell are you doing here?'

'Can't you see? I was sleeping!'

Louise squirmed free of Taillefer's grip. The sun was back,

and she felt energised by the prospect of a bright day ahead. She sprang up and took a few steps across the parquet. The house was even more welcoming by daylight, with the living space extending out onto a terrace surrounded by a small garden.

'How did you get back from the hospital?'

'In a taxi.'

'You should have rung me. I'd have come to get you.'

'In your little sardine tin? Really not my bag.'

He tilted his chin at her cello, which he'd placed on an armchair.

'You left your keys in the ignition, I'll have you know, with *that* thing still inside. Honestly, are you living in Muppet land?'

'Oh well. It seems pretty quiet round here. Where's Muppet land, anyway?'

'Don't judge by appearances. Ever. And answer me this: why did you sleep here?'

'Because I was tired,' she shrugged.

Taillefer turned puce.

'Why did you sleep *here*? IN MY HOUSE!'

'OK, keep your hair on! I fed your dog – like you asked me to – and then I dozed off. No need to blow your top.'

'Do you live with your dad? Let him know where you are, he'll be worried.'

Louise shook her head, stifling a yawn.

'I have a student room in Rue des Carmes. My dad lives in the Alps with his wife and her two kids. I'll text him later.'

She stretched and caught sight of the clock.

'I hadn't realised it was already lunchtime! I don't suppose there's any hope of a bite to eat . . . ?'

The cop let out a sigh, but strained to keep his cool. After all, he was hungry too, and there were a few questions he wanted to ask Louise.

The young woman followed him into the kitchen. Set around a large Corian island unit, the room mirrored the colour scheme of the living area, with oiled oak bar stools complementing the creamy palette.

'What do you fancy?' he asked.

'Any chance of pasta?' she ventured, perching on a stool.

'Will carbonara do you?'

'Sure!'

2

'So, did you investigate my mum's death?'

After setting a large pan of water to boil, Taillefer began lining up his ingredients next to the induction hob.

'"Investigate" is a big word. I did what I'd promised you: I read everything I could find, took stock of the facts and spoke with the cop who led the team that attended the scene.'

'And what was the upshot?'

Taillefer took a bowl and cracked three eggs into it, saving only the yolks, which he mixed with a grating of parmesan.

'Why do you think your mum was murdered?'

Slightly wrongfooted, Louise was forced to admit that she didn't have any solid reasons.

'Call it a hunch.'

Taillefer rolled his eyes heavenwards.

'A hunch means nothing!'

'If that's all you can tell me, thanks for your help.'

'I'm going to tell you something else – in no uncertain terms: your mum had more than a gram of alcohol in her blood, and she was using her balcony as a weed farm.'

'So . . . ?'

'So, she wasn't exactly a model of stability.'

'And your next point . . . ?'

'Just think for a minute: who'd stand to gain from her death?'

Louise gave a theatrical shrug.

'Did you check her bank accounts?' he pressed.

'They were almost empty. At the top of her career, a prima ballerina can earn about seven thousand euros, but my mum spent money as quickly as she earnt it. She hadn't even finished paying off her flat.'

'Who'll inherit it? You?'

'Yeah, through an emancipation order. Provided my dad helps me clear the rest of the mortgage.'

'Talking of your dad, what was his relationship with her like?'

'Non-existent. They split up when I was five. Living with Stella Petrenko was no picnic.'

'Why?' he asked, continuing to pummel his egg mix.

'My dad often says that a prima ballerina is someone who only listens when the conversation revolves around her. That's obviously an exaggeration, but in my mum's case, I can't say he was wrong.'

As the water began to boil, Taillefer tossed in a palmful of salt and dunked his tagliatelle into the pan.

'I loved my mum,' Louise went on, keen to clarify herself, 'but she was selfish, unhappy and made life difficult for everyone around her. She was a fighter, but I think she'd taken too many knocks to find any real contentment.'

'Was there a man in her life, at the time of her death?'

'Not just *one*, dozens. She fell in love with a different guy every week.'

'Aren't you overdoing it a bit?'

'No, that's partly why she was so unstable: her obsession with being in love.'

Not to mention her insatiable need for sex . . .

Taillefer splashed some oil into a frying pan to brown his chunks of guanciale.

'Did you ever wonder if she might kill herself?'

Louise shrugged again.

'My mum was far too narcissistic for that.'

'Even so, the cop I spoke with said she was wearing her full stage get-up – leotard, stockings, tutu. Doesn't that feel like a kind of last hurrah?'

'No, it was something she did a lot. She'd kept up her training routine and the habit of dressing in her old tutus – sometimes she even wore them during the day.'

'OK, what's your theory, then?'

'What theory?'

'How do you explain your mum being murdered when the door to the flat was locked from inside?'

'The roof,' Louise replied matter-of-factly. 'Someone sneaked onto the roof and surprised her by jumping onto the balcony. She had a little terrace up there, and in summer she'd take her chair out and spend all day reading or scrolling on her phone.'

'Supposing that's plausible, it still doesn't explain the motive.'

'I thought you'd understood.'

'Understood what?'

'The motive's precisely what I'd like you to help me find!'

3

Louise devoured her mound of pasta in under three minutes. To make the most of the sunshine, Taillefer had laid the outside table and fired up a restaurant-style chiminea.

'I'm honoured by your respect for my cooking.'

He finished his own plate in silence while the young woman resumed her efforts to keep him on the case.

'*At least* come and see the flat so you can judge for yourself. I can drive you there after lunch.'

'Three months on from the event, it won't achieve much. Anyway, I have an important meeting this afternoon.'

'Tomorrow, then!'

'Not tomorrow, not ever.'

'The day after tomorrow?'

'You must have cloth ears, I swear . . .'

He cleared the table and returned with two espressos.

'Here's some advice for you,' he said as he sat back down. 'Move on. Your mum's dead, it's sad, but accept it. And believe me, a half-baked detective game isn't going to bring her back.'

Louise leapt to her feet and began pacing the terrace.

'I'm not giving up now,' she insisted. 'I'll see this through to the end, with or without your help. There are private investigators who . . .'

'That's right, fritter away your poxy inheritance on some

private eye. Very smart idea. Clearly you're not so clever after all.'

'Help me, then! Bloody well help me!'

Taillefer contained his annoyance, letting out a lengthy sigh. Struggling to see against the glare, he reached for his smoke-lens sunglasses, then crossed his legs on the table and sparked up.

'You really are brain-dead to smoke with your heart condition. Tobacco raises your blood pressure and it clogs your arteries. You're killing yourself with every puff. It makes me sick!'

The cop made no response. He carried on soaking up the rays and took another voluptuous gulp of tar-stained air. He felt like sticking two fingers up at everything. For days he'd felt keyed-up, mired in a hole he couldn't haul himself out of. He knew the reason: it was the twenty-eighth of December. A symbolic date in his life. A date that cast him back to a time of happiness, togetherness and hope, but which today loomed ahead of him with a sense of dread that – clichéd though it was – wrenched at his heart. It would be a long day. He'd turn up for his meeting at 4 p.m. He'd drag things out to avoid getting home too early. Then, once he was back, he'd drain a bottle and swallow a benzo to black out as fast as possible. He'd do the same the next day. And the day after that. Running away. Into sleep, dreams, and oblivion. Too bad if his heart gave up on him. Maybe that would even be for the best . . .

'Are we off then, Mathias? Shall I give you a lift there?'

Standing over him, the little nuisance was back on the case. There was only one reason he hadn't sent her packing already. In some way, she was a distraction. By keeping him on his toes, she stopped him sinking altogether.

'Have you abandoned your private detective plan?'

'I want you to do it. How many more times!'

'Listen, you don't know me. I've already told you, I'm not a nice guy. You're seventeen years old. You've grown up in a privileged bubble and you don't have a clue how dangerous the world can be. You shouldn't trust people just because you find them friendly.'

'I don't find you remotely friendly, I promise you that.'

'You seem like a bright girl, so I'll say this one last time – loud and clear: you're in danger if you stay with me.'

She eyed him doubtfully. She'd instinctively assumed the opposite. He wasn't a man who inspired suspicion or a fear of dirty tricks. He came across as a shield, a defender who could block the arrows and the blows should anyone try to hurt her.

'Don't trust your hunches,' he reminded her, as though reading her thoughts.

'All right, Mr Lofty Pronouncements,' she snorted, turning off the chiminea.

'Hey, switch that back on!'

'No way. This thing's an environmental disaster.'

'At least it stops us freezing our arses off.'

'We might not be "freezing our arses off", but we're destroying the planet.'

'Wiping out humanity, at most.'

'And that's not an issue for you?'

'That would suit me nicely, actually. The planet will rock along just fine without us.'

'You're pathetic,' she replied. 'Anyway, are you helping me or not? We're going round in circles here.'

Taillefer hesitated for the final time. What if – just maybe – fate had sent the girl his way as a sign? Or as an instrument . . .

'I'll come to see your mum's flat. But in return, I want you to do something for me.'

'Again? What is it this time?'

'And I want it done with no questions asked.'

'It's a deal.'

4

7th arrondissement
Saint-Thomas-d'Aquin quarter

Louise parked up the voiturette between an Italian furniture shop and the new Yves Saint Laurent HQ in the former Cistercian convent of Pentemont Abbey. Stella Petrenko's flat was in an attractive Haussmann-style mansion, at the intersection of Rue de Bellechasse and Rue Las-Cases. Taillefer peered up to assess the property. It was an impressive edifice, built in the distinctive creamy Saint-Maximin limestone that since the eighteenth century had fashioned some of the capital's most handsome addresses. Dragging his leg, still feeling battered by his heart scare, he followed Louise into the entrance hall. The space was decked in gilding, with wide quartz floor tiles and a huge lantern chandelier. They passed the caretaker's lodge, which, belying its advertised opening hours, was deserted, then headed for the lift to the fifth floor.

'I've left everything how it was,' Louise warned as she pushed open the door.

Stella Petrenko's hideaway was a little corner apartment, with a square floor plan and pastel-tone décor. A large mirror behind a training barre gave the living area an appealing sense of breadth, while the view over the Paris rooftops perfected the romantic cocoon vibe.

The place was as Taillefer had imagined it. He could tell the dancer had tried to recreate the feel of an opera-house dressing room. She'd thought of it all – from the collection of ballet pumps strung from hooks, to the leotard-and-tutu-clad mannequins, right down to the velvet wing chair that could have been straight from a François Boucher painting. Behind an ornate wooden dressing table, a whole wall had been plastered with postcards and tributes from fans, alongside photos of ballet masters, pianists and celebrities. Among them Taillefer recognised Pina Bausch and Béjart, as well as an ageing Rudolf Nureyev receiving an honour from the former president Sarkozy.

Opening the French windows, Louise invited Taillefer to join her on the scene of the supposed crime. The balcony area was unconventional, more redolent of a small terrace with its indoor-outdoor configuration. The original space had been reworked with a frosted-glass canopy, held aloft by wrought-iron brackets that were twined with Virginia creeper. Flowerpots lined the parapet, though their contents had withered in the cold, while an array of terracotta planters hung from the flaking paintwork of the high wooden shutters. Abandoned in a corner, a greying teak stepladder looked as if it had been frozen in place.

Taillefer leant over the balustrade, which was as low and rusty as Fatoumata Diop had described. He glanced up to survey the roof. Provided you were light and nimble, it

35

would theoretically be possible to gain access to the terrace, but he couldn't see it. What thief would attempt something so risky, only to leave empty-handed? And if the dancer had confronted the intruder, there would have been signs of a struggle. It made no sense. The most likely scenario was the one that Diop's team had settled on: having drunk herself stupid, Petrenko had climbed the stepladder to water her plants, and had taken a final, ill-judged swan dive. He shared his thoughts with Louise, who threw him a reproachful look.

A dazzling flash struck Taillefer's face. Across the street, someone had opened or closed a window, and the glass had reflected the sunlight in a mirror effect. The cop shielded his eyes with his hand. The apartment block opposite – a series of three white, six-storey buildings – was a hive of potential witnesses, yet to his knowledge no had come forward with any interesting leads.

Leaving the French windows ajar, he returned inside to poke his head in the bathroom, still in search of an improbable clue. In the medicine cabinet, he found some condoms and a stash of his old friends, benzodiazepine and sertraline. Inevitably, the wings were less edifying than the stage. He felt a sudden wave of revulsion. What was he doing here, sniffing around someone else's dirty laundry like a sordid gawker?

He headed back to the living room, where Louise was waiting for him. To leave no stone unturned, he combed through the items on the desk: a pebbled-leather diary, a mobile phone, an Anna Akhmatova poetry collection, a pearl-encrusted Zippo, a novel that he flipped open on a page carrying the underlined quote: *'Love has no age limit.*

What does have a limit – and an expiry date – is being loved.' He thumbed the diary distractedly as he paced up and down the flat. He wasn't sure what to think. He scanned the space, clocking details as he'd done hundreds of times back in his police days, hoping for a spark of inspiration, some link with a previously gleaned lead. He cocked his ear, listening for the murmur of the street below, the muffled growl of the lift, a phantom noise in the corridor.

As he looked up, a small canvas on the wall caught his eye. It showed a young man with silvery, pupilless eyes, outlined against a turquoise background. The subject's delicate features, coupled with his empty zombie eyes, were somehow both captivating and nightmarish.

'Do you know who painted this?'

'No,' Louise replied. 'It hasn't been there long.'

'And is that your mum's phone?'

She nodded.

'Do you know her password?'

'No, but I was thinking maybe you could . . .'

'Forget that. I'm useless with technology. You'll be more clued-up than me on that front, guaranteed.'

The sound of the doorbell interrupted their conversation. Having spotted them as they came in, the caretaker had pounced on the chance to bring Louise a bundle of post. Taillefer hung back from the exchange. He couldn't keep his eyes off the portrait of the young zombie. The art that people owned said a lot about them. Spending years living with a painting was no innocent occurrence. The choice itself betrayed something about your personality. Then, once it was hanging in place, its presence permeated you day by day, seeping under your skin, for better or for worse.

As the canvas wasn't signed on the front, he unhooked it from the wall to read the label on the back of the frame.

```
Marco Sabatini
Soldier #96
Bernard Benedick Gallery
125 Rue du Faubourg-Saint-Honoré
```

He jotted down the details, then, returning his gaze to the room, collared the caretaker before she disappeared.

5

'Good afternoon, madam. Captain Taillefer, Major Crime Unit. Could you spare me five minutes?'

She eyed him suspiciously, wheeling out the classic: 'I already told your colleagues everything three months ago.' Sensing she was poised to demand his badge, the ex-cop composed his features and put on his syrupiest voice.

'The examining magistrate has ordered some further enquiries before we close the case. It won't take long.'

With a smile, he beckoned her to take a seat across the desk from him. To complete his old-school performance, he plucked one of the pens from the tabletop and began taking notes on an old writing pad that the dancer had brought back from Hotel Normandy.

'Your name, please?'

'Myriam Morlino. I look after three blocks of flats in the street – number twenty-seven, number twenty-nine and number thirty-one.'

'Is your office in this building?'

'No, next door. There used to be two caretakers, but the owners wanted to cut costs – you know how it is.'

'Did you know Stella Petrenko well?'

'Fairly well. I've only been here since January, but Ms Petrenko often chatted to me. You can ask Mrs Mertens, too – she was the old caretaker.'

'I will. On the evening of the accident, didn't you hear anything?'

'No, I go to bed early. But I've already said all this.'

Myriam Morlino fanned the outsized tunic she was wearing, as if starved of air despite the chill of the room.

'Who called the ambulance?'

'The owner of 9 Thermidor, the bar on the corner. He was just closing up when she fell.'

'Who were the last people to see her alive?'

'I don't know,' she replied tetchily. 'It didn't seem like she was getting out much those last months. On the day it happened, I dropped off her post at elevenish, the same as every morning, then a nurse stopped by later in the afternoon.'

'A nurse?'

'To change her dressings, after her surgery.'

Taillefer turned to Louise with a frown.

'What surgery?'

She dismissed the question with a flick of the hand.

'Just a routine procedure, I'll explain later.'

Taillefer remembered seeing the details of a nursing firm scrawled in the dancer's diary. He leafed back through until he located the address:

Nora Messaoud Nursing Practice
35 Rue de Bourgogne
75007 Paris

He tore out the page and stuffed it in his pocket before resuming his questioning.

'As far as you know, was Stella Petrenko taking anything other than weed and medication? Were there any dealers who used to stop by?'

'Hey, that's out of order!' Louise protested.

'God knows,' the caretaker replied. 'She had a lot of men around the place, but I don't think they were dealing drugs.'

'Who were they, then?'

Morlino looked slightly uncomfortable.

'Visitors, relatives . . .'

'Lovers?' Taillefer pressed.

'Yes, most likely,' she admitted. 'Getting older didn't seem easy for Ms Petrenko. It reassured her when men still found her attractive – even if, as time went on, it was more a case of quantity over quality . . .' She glanced at Louise. 'No offence intended, miss.'

'Who else lives in the building, Mrs Morlino?'

The caretaker scowled and gave a long sigh of exasperation, as if replying to Taillefer's question required a superhuman effort.

'On the ground floor there's a solicitor's office belonging to a couple called the Lamberts, who also have a duplex on the first and second floor. Doctor Rolland has his practice on the third floor, as well as a private flat, and the fourth floor is owned by Americans, but they only come in the spring.'

'And up here, on the fifth floor?'

'Ms Petrenko, obviously, then there's another little flat where the painter from upstairs used to store his material.'

'And upstairs, I presume that's where the old servants' rooms are?'

'Yes, but they've all been knocked through into one big studio.'

'Who owns that?'

'Marco Sabatini, a young Italian artist – the one I just mentioned. He's the one who painted that,' she said, nodding at the portrait that Taillefer had taken down from the wall.

The cop's eyes lit up.

'Is he in his studio now? I'd be keen to ask him a few questions.'

'You'll have your work cut out.'

'Why?'

'Because he's dead.'

'Since when?'

'Last summer, from Covid. At least, that's what they said, but . . .'

She left the unfinished sentence hanging in the air.

'But what?' Taillefer urged.

'If you ask me, it was more like the vaccine that killed him.'

'The Covid vaccine?'

'Don't you know what that thing contains? Tiny little particles of graphene oxide. And you know why? To control us all remotely with 5G chips.'

For a moment Taillefer thought she was joking. But no, Myriam Morlino was deadly serious – and she wasn't done yet.

'They use the graphene to magnetise us, to make us do whatever they want. Then the blood clots and stops flowing to the heart and brain. My sister-in-law knows someone who died from it – after their electromagnetic field had been tampered with.'

'That's rubbish!' Louise objected. 'I'm a medical student and what you're saying is dangerous, believe me.'

'No, you couldn't be more wrong. People call us conspiracy theorists, but we're the ones with our heads screwed on. Once most of the population has been vaccinated, they'll start sending out waves through people's phones, then the particles will grow and give birth to THE THING – a kind of alien that will take over everyone's bodies.'

Louise abandoned her arguments and stared at Myriam Morlino in consternation. Taillefer had stopped listening. With age, he'd become pathologically intolerant to imbecility. He checked his watch. He absolutely couldn't be late for his meeting.

'We've heard enough,' he told Louise. 'Let's go.'

Before they left, he slipped the Marco Sabatini canvas into a Repetto tote bag that he'd spotted under the desk.

'Why are you taking that?' Louise asked.

'Because it's evidence. And because I like it.'

4

AN UNREASONABLE TIME

1

Place de la Concorde

As the voiturette zigzagged through the Paris traffic, Taillefer shrank into the passenger seat feeling as if he'd been strapped inside a plastic washtub. After passing the Fontaine des Mers and the obelisk, Louise switched on the hazard lights to pull up on the forecourt of the Big Wheel. Taillefer barely waited for the car to stop before opening the door and diving out to shake his seized-up legs. Louise caught up with him by the entrance to the ride, which had been back in its festive home since the end of November.

'I've always hated this thing,' she grumbled, gesturing at the wheel.

'It wasn't my choice to meet here.'

'Who are you meeting? An eight-year-old?'

He shook his head noncommittally.

'I'm early. Do you want a waffle?'

'All we do is eat with you, Taillefer. I'll have gained a stone by the end of this investigation.'

The cop made his way towards the waffle stall, from which a pleasing smell of mulled wine was wafting. Barging aside an indecisive teenager, he headed straight for the counter to order a cone of churros, while Louise succumbed to a crêpe. As their order was being prepared, he slunk aside to take out the page he'd ripped from Stella Petrenko's diary, uncrumpling it to read the number the dancer had scrawled. He was keen to verify the nurse story. Hearing the answering machine of Nora Messaoud's practice, he asked them to call him back urgently.

'Let's divvy up the tasks,' he suggested as Louise joined him with her crêpe. 'After my meeting, I'll find a way to speak to the nurse before the end of the day. In the meantime, I'd like you to visit the gallery where Marco Sabatini's paintings are exhibited.'

'Why?' she asked, keeping one eye on the hastily parked voiturette.

'Because this thing about the painter who died of Covid is interesting.'

'How's it relevant to my mum's death?'

'A hunch.'

'I thought hunches meant nothing.'

'Cut the cheek and do what I'm asking you. Two deaths in the same building in the space of a few days are worth checking out.'

'You still haven't said what you want me to do in return for your help with the investigation.'

'I'm coming to that. But first, just so we're clear: I explain, and you do it. No questions, no smart-alec comments, got it?'

44

She nodded. Taillefer pressed on.

'There's an Italian restaurant near Place Furstemberg called the Number 6.'

'I think I know the one.'

'Get there for 7 p.m. this evening, sit down at the bar and order a drink. Nothing alcoholic, eh? I don't want you getting in any trouble. From there, you'll have a view across the room.'

'And then what?'

'Keep your eyes peeled for a pretty, Lebanese-looking woman in her forties.'

'Who is she?'

'We agreed no questions.'

Louise was tempted to crack a joke, but something told her that wouldn't be wise.

'If you see her, take a picture on your phone and send it to me.'

'Is that all?'

'That's all.'

'Will she be alone?'

'If she comes, yes.'

'How long should I wait?'

'Forty-five minutes. An hour, tops.'

'Gotcha.'

'We'll keep in touch, OK?' Taillefer added, jiggling his phone.

As he began to walk away, she sped after him.

'Wait, what should I ask the Marco Sabatini gallery owner?'

As he turned around, Mathias was struck once more by the young woman's keen, anxious gaze.

'I don't know, but you're bright enough to think of something.'

He spun away, leaving Louise with her questions. She watched him for a moment as he strode off, soon to be joined by a tall figure wearing a red parka with a fur-lined hood. She squinted to get a better view of the stranger, but a second later, the two men were swallowed by the crowd.

2

Bernard Benedick Gallery was in a large unit in Rue du Faubourg Saint-Honoré. Despite the stark lighting, Louise thought at first that it was closed. There was no sign of life through the window. She tried the buzzer anyway, and a few moments later the door clicked open. A young woman with short hair, piercings, visible tattoos and a black-and-white 'Justice for Adama' T-shirt came to meet her.

'Can I help you?'

'I'd like to talk to Bernard Benedick.'

The gallery assistant blinked behind her oversized glasses.

'Talk to him about what?' she asked, with a hint of condescension.

'About this painting,' Louise replied, producing from the tote bag the small canvas that Taillefer had taken from her mother's flat.

The girl changed her tune instantly.

'Oh, a Sabatini! That's a wonderful example you have there! The bright-blue background is the most sought-after, along with the pink. I'll get Mr Benedick. You're in luck

– he only got back from New York this morning, and he's off to San José tomorrow.'

Once she was alone again, Louise wondered what the hell she was doing there, unable to shake a creeping sense of unease. Though she was pleased with how Taillefer's involvement had gone so far, the painting lead seemed a long way from her main concern, and she had no idea how she could move the investigation along.

'. . . *you're bright enough to think of something.*'

Fuck you, Taillefer!

While she waited for Bernard Benedick, Louise wandered through the gallery. The first two rooms housed an exhibition entitled 'White Noise', a collective project centred on the colour white – white monochromes, marble sculptures, a blanched-linen tapestry depicting an ethereal, silent snowscape. On one of the walls, in large letters, a flashing white neon light proclaimed: 'Down with the white rot'. Louise felt slightly queasy. The whole collection made her think of a giant, frosted vat of concentrated milk. Unsettling and unsavoury.

She found refuge in the final room, which proved much more interesting. Under the title of 'The Army of the Dead', the exhibition brought together twenty or so portraits by Marco Sabatini. The paintings followed a common theme, foregrounding the same face of a young man with hollow, silvery pupils, fixing the observer with his zombie-like stare. Only the background changed each time. Some were richly textured, featuring sand dunes, jungles and mountains, while others comprised flat blocks of rich colour. The light was never the same either, sweeping the spectrum from falling dusk to the pale glow of winter dawns. Each scene was

47

charged with tension, as if some unknown drama were simmering beneath the surface, as if struggle, blood and death were never far away.

'Remarkable work, isn't it?'

The question sprang Louise from her thoughts. She turned to greet Bernard Benedick. With his orange jumper, skinny jeans and gaudy trainers, the sixty-something had clearly gambled on the youthful card.

'What can I do for you?'

Louise showed him the painting, explaining that she'd found it in the flat of her mother, the prima ballerina Stella Petrenko.

'Yes, of course. We framed and delivered it ourselves. In the 7th arrondissement, if I remember rightly . . . ?'

Louise nodded.

'The artist gave it to your mother as a gift. From what I understood, the two of them were neighbours and got along well.'

The gallery owner's round, affable eyes twinkled through his Le Corbusier glasses.

'If your mum's looking to sell the painting, I'll happily buy it back off her.'

'My mother's dead.'

'Oh, gosh, I . . . I'm sorry. I've really put my foot in it. I'm often away abroad and I hadn't—'

'Don't worry about it,' Louise cut in.

'Can I get you a coffee? Or something else?'

'Just some water, please, if you have it.'

Benedick invited her to follow him to his office, which was on a mezzanine accessed by an industrial metal staircase. Inside, the gallery owner had created a simple lounge area with a clear acrylic table and two squat armchairs.

'Still or sparkling?'

'Still, please. Could you tell me a bit more about Marco Sabatini's paintings?'

'With pleasure,' Benedick replied, still embarrassed by his blunder. 'When he died, Marco had just celebrated his thirty-first birthday. He trained in Milan, at the Brera Fine Arts Academy. He was what we call an "emerging artist". We started displaying his paintings two years ago – first as part of group exhibitions, then, after his work was well received, this year we took the plunge and organised a solo show around his self-portraits. "The Army of the Dead" is the name he gave to the collection himself.'

'Did you know him well?'

'Not really. He was an extremely private, introverted artist, who rarely left his studio. He never did publicity events and he was very detached from the business side of things. We had minimal contact with him, despite selling a lot of his work at Art Paris, FIAC and Art Basel. In commercial terms, his death's been a real blow for us.'

'I get the impression he always painted the same scene. Is that right?'

'Yes, spot on. Always the same tormented figure, just with minor variations that collectors of his work get very excited about.'

'Is there some message behind it all?'

'I don't know. He wasn't the type to discuss his work. But . . .' The gallery owner stood up to retrieve a booklet from the shelf.

'. . . we did do a brochure about his last exhibition. The curator who wrote the texts draws a parallel between the

49

zombification process and modern-day Haitian voodoo rituals. You should have a read – it's fascinating. Here you go, you're welcome to keep it.'

'Thanks,' Louise replied, slightly bewildered.

'I sometimes wonder if Sabatini would have been capable of painting anything else. Sadly, we'll never know.'

'Did he really die of Covid?'

'Yes, that's what they said in the press. And his fiancée told me the same when she came to bring me three of the paintings he'd finished just before he died. It's mad, he was so young . . .'

'Do you know anything about his relationship with my mother?'

Bernard Benedick looked pained.

'I wish I could help you, but I'm afraid I don't know anything else.'

3

Place de la Contrescarpe
5th arrondissement

I've just arrived in the bar, the text message announced.

Taillefer looked up towards the entrance and spotted Nora Messaoud. The nurse certainly had style: fitted beige trench coat, long, straightened black hair, bright-red lipstick. He motioned to her to join him at his table by the back wall.

'Thank you for coming. Would you like anything?'

'No, thanks,' she replied, sitting her bag on the edge of the table. 'I've still got at least another two hours until I clock off. If I start on the Moscow Mules now, it could be fatal.'

A series of lightning flashes strobed through the café, followed by the deep rumble of thunder. Flopping into the vacant chair, Nora glanced at her watch and had a partial change of heart.

'Actually, I wouldn't say no to a mint Perrier with ice and two slices of lemon – as long as they make it quick.'

Taillefer manhandled a passing waiter to place the order.

'I didn't understand a word of what you said over the phone, Inspector Taillefer.'

'Captain,' he corrected.

'If you insist, *Capitán!*'

'The Major Crime Unit has taken over the investigation into Stella Petrenko's death.'

'Major Crime, seriously?'

'Just a few routine checks before the file's closed.'

'And what's that got to do with me?'

'You saw her the day she died, didn't you?'

'That's right. I changed her dressings for over a month.'

'What was wrong with her?'

'Dupuytren's contracture. Do you know what it is?'

'Not a clue.'

'It's a condition affecting the tissues in the palm and fingers.'

As she spoke, Nora Messaoud demonstrated on her own hand joints. She had exceedingly long, scarlet fingernails, with the tips filed into stiletto-sharp points.

'The symptoms start off mild, but they get worse with age. Over time, the affected tissues stiffen to form nodules in the palm and very thick cords, which gradually contract to shut down movement in the fingers.'

'What causes it?'

Messaoud shrugged and took a slug of her drink.

'We're not too sure. There's definitely a genetic link, because it often affects several members of the same family. Alcohol and smoking seem to be risk factors too.'

Taillefer couldn't stop looking at the nurse's hands. Each nail was different, painstakingly embellished with a tiny motif – a star, a flower, a butterfly, a crescent moon. The razorlike talons had an almost supernatural hold over him.

'Is it painful?' he asked.

'Not really, but eventually it becomes very incapacitating – enough to need surgery.'

'Is that what happened with Stella Petrenko?'

'Yes, she had to undergo a total removal of the abnormal tissues – the hard cords I mentioned.'

'On both hands?'

The nurse thought for a moment.

'No, it was only the right one. Luckily for her, Stella was left-handed.'

'Are you sure?'

'Positive.'

'So she'd have been fine holding a full watering can in her good hand?'

'I don't see why not. Actually, do you mind if I go out for a smoke?'

Taillefer accompanied her to the small canopy where the other nicotine addicts were huddled, sheltering from the rain-slicked square. It was months since he'd set foot in the Latin Quarter. He distantly recalled Place de la Contrescarpe in the springtime, with its quaint village-square feel that was a world away from the dismal late-December scene. The place looked bald. Two of the four trees around the central fountain had been cut down, and in the gap the council had installed a reclaimed-plywood cone as an eco-friendly alternative to the traditional Christmas tree. As an afterthought, the pallets had been sellotaped with a cheap string of fairy lights that flooded the square in tacky white light.

'I've always wondered why people let their cities be defaced like this,' Nora remarked.

Taillefer agreed, but dodged the topic to keep his investigation in view.

'So, your role was managing Stella Petrenko's post-op care?'

'Essentially, but there wasn't a lot to it. She had to wear a splint for the first couple of weeks, and then it was a case of changing the dressings regularly.'

'Every day?'

'Yes, to stop it getting infected.'

'And you saw her every day for about a month.'

'That's right.' Nora let out a long puff of smoke.

'What did she talk to you about?'

'Nothing much. It's a quick job, you know, changing that kind of dressing. I rarely stayed more than ten minutes.'

'What was your impression of her?'

'My daughter does ballet, so obviously I was intrigued to meet Stella. She gave me one of her old kit bags to pass on, which was nice.'

'I found a stash of Lexapro and Zoloft in the bathroom. Was she depressed?'

'Aren't we all?' Nora asked with a smile.

Taillefer frowned.

'You know what I mean.'

53

'Yeah, I'd say she wasn't in great shape. She didn't like getting older – not being the star she once was.'

'Did she have lovers?'

'I reckon she shagged anything she could find.'

'Did she discuss them with you?'

'Not really, I'm just being a cow,' Nora replied, checking her watch. 'Right, Captain, if you're done with me, I'll get back to the coalface. Thanks for the drink.'

Nora Messaoud tossed her cigarette butt in the gutter, and with a backwards wave she was gone.

4

Ducking back inside the bar, Taillefer slapped a note on the counter and left without waiting for the change. He sloped through the drizzle to the taxi rank in Place Monge, where he climbed into a cab and gave his address, then asked the driver to turn off the radio that was blaring through the passenger compartment.

With the return of the dark and rain, he'd already put up a wall between himself and the world, dreading the lonely misery of the evening ahead. He stared out of the window, barely registering the deserted streets as they flashed past, when suddenly his phone sounded.

FaceTime call from Louise Collange.

With a knot of apprehension, he picked up the grainy image of the young woman sitting at the dimly lit bar of the Number 6.

'Well, your friend isn't here. I'll give it a bit longer and then I'm off, OK?'

Mathias gave no reply. What he saw on the screen stoked painful memories. He still recalled the décor – the terracotta floor, red-brick walls and exposed oak beams. The muted yet warm lighting. The nonna-style ravioli to die for.

Louise filled him in on her fruitless visit to the gallery, then he related his meeting with the nurse. There were no two ways about it. The start of their investigation had hit a brick wall.

'I did tell you,' he began, 'your mum—'

'You're a pain in the arse!' she retorted, before cutting the call dead.

A heavy sigh. The cobbles of Square de Montsouris. The house. The comforting presence of Titus. Mathias locked the door behind him and didn't even bother to turn the lights on. He took off his shoes in the dark, then went through the same mechanical motions to feed the dog. Returning to the living room, he groped for the bottle of Karuizawa, flumped onto the sofa and took a first long swig. His inability to hold his drink was probably what had saved him from becoming an alcoholic, and the whisky soon knocked him senseless.

Bedlam.

He closed his eyes and let the day's events churn through his mind. The halo of pale light around Louise Collange's pensive face. The zombified stare of Marco Sabatini's paintings. The caretaker's bulging eyes and features warped by conspiracy-theorist logorrhoea. The mysterious conversation he'd had in the Big Wheel on Place de la Concorde. Lena who hadn't shown up at the Number 6. Nora Messaoud's stiletto fingernails.

By now Taillefer had detached from reality. In his nightmare, the nurse's long nails were clawing at his throat. Blood was draining out of him, but he felt no pain. He was lying on a battlefield, between two trenches, while crows circled overhead. Sitting on top of him, her legs straddling his body, the nurse continued to sink in her talons, this time slashing at his stomach. But when he looked closer, he realised it wasn't Nora, but Myriam Morlino, the caretaker from Rue de Bellechasse.

'Watch out for the graphene! They're trying to steal control of your mind!'

He was covered in blood, his head throbbing as if someone had stabbed a knitting needle through his ears. Morlino grabbed him by the hair and jerked his head back and forth.

'Your phone's ringing, you fool!' she screeched. 'It's THE THING!'

Taillefer woke up wet with sweat. *Shit* . . . His heart was hammering. Titus had jumped onto his face and was slavering over his nose and mouth. He wiped himself down with his sleeve before picking up. It wasn't The Thing. It was Nora Messaoud.

'All right, Captain? From your breathing, it sounds like I've caught you in the middle of a workout. Or rolling in the hay.'

'Neither, as it happens,' he replied. 'I was having a nightmare.'

'Already in bed at half-nine? You're quite the wild one, aren't you!'

He scratched Titus's head before staggering to his feet.

'Anyway,' the nurse continued, 'I'm calling because something else occurred to me. It's probably not important.'

Taillefer's ears pricked up.

'Go on.'

56

'I told you I saw Stella Petrenko every day for a month. That isn't quite true. At the end of August, about ten days before she died, I went on holiday for a week and as often happens, the clinic hired an agency nurse to cover for me.'

The cop massaged his temples, not sure if he'd understood.

'So during that week, another nurse came to change Stella's dressings. Is that what you're saying?'

'Yes, from 25 August to 1 September.'

'Could you find her name for me?'

'I've already looked it up, actually.'

Taillefer scrambled for a pen.

'She was called Charvet,' Nora announced. 'Angélique Charvet.'

The nurse left a pause before chancing her luck.

'I've just finished my shift. Would you fancy taking me for sushi? I know a great place in the 8th arrondissement . . .'

II

ANGÉLIQUE CHARVET

5

THE TWO SIDES OF THE TRACKS

Four months earlier
The Paris suburbs
28 August

1

My name is Angélique Charvet.
  Thirty-four years old.
  Sitting over the toilet bowl.
  With a pregnancy test in my hand.
  Positive.

2

The two lines on the plastic stick seem to be goading me.
It's not like I hadn't seen them coming, though. Late period,
tender breasts, repeated waves of morning sickness. Getting

to my feet, I fling the test in the sink and dive into the shower.

As I stand under the scalding water, I try to track back to identify 'the father'. Mentally, I rewind the days and the weeks . . . until I hit on Corentin Lelièvre. A shitty Tinder date at the start of August that I'd already half blanked out. A small-time freelance hack who presented himself as a 'militant journalist' working on the activist fringes of the establishment press. Moon-face like Gaston Lagaffe, goatee beard, and a receding hairline he desperately attempted to hide under a wide-brimmed baseball cap. A roundabout way of saying he looked nothing like his profile pictures.

He'd taken me to the Enfants Terribles, a bar on Quai de Jemmapes. He was wearing a pathetic eco-warrior T-shirt with the slogan: 'There is no planet B'. The guy had opinions about everything. He was so hooked on the sound of his own voice that I'd zoned out within fifteen minutes. And downed a lot of lemon drops. I must have had one too many. Otherwise I'd never have agreed to go back to his flat in Rue Eugène-Varlin. In bed, he'd kept up his mediocre standards. That's when the condom must have broken. Although it wasn't the size of his dick that did it.

I get out of the shower and throw on my clothes. Try not to think of that loser who's brought me back up against my own stupidity. I'll sort it out like last time. A visit to Sophie Charbonnier's clinic in Rue du Cherche-Midi. Sophie was in my first-year nursing class in Bordeaux, back in our uni days. She's a mile up her own arse, but she'll spare me the psychological crap. A mifepristone pill to terminate the pregnancy, then a dose of misoprostol thirty-six hours later.

It won't be pretty, but at least by next weekend the problem will be behind me.

3

Aulnay-sous-Bois
8 a.m.

The heavens have opened as I leave the crumbling burrstone block where I've been living since arriving in Paris eight years ago. It's the twenty-eighth of August. Summer's in full swing all over the whole country, except in the shithole that is Île-de-France. I head past the roundabout at Place du Général-Leclerc, onto Boulevard de Strasbourg, then up Route de Bondy to the station. What's more depressing than the suburban wastelands of Seine-Saint-Denis? Seine-Saint-Denis in the rain.

It's the usual anarchy to catch the RER B. The train is sweating. Literally. A tropical heat has leached into the carriages, making the ride into Paris even rougher than normal. I flick open Instagram. The girls are in Corsica, Saint-Tropez, Tuscany, posing in stunning hotels on the Adriatic Coast. My timeline's an explosion of Mediterranean colour. A riot of sea, sunglasses, hot sand, glasses of spritz, flamingo pool floats. *#summer #goodvibes #sun #love #holidays #naturelover #hotsummernight #summerbliss #protectyourskin #beachbabe #bikiniseason*. The hashtags on my screen are countered by the station names flashing past my window. Drancy, La Courneuve, Gare-du-Nord, Châtelet-Les-Halles. A change at Saint-Michel-Notre-Dame before my final destination.

Emerging from Musée d'Orsay station feels like a deliverance. At last, I can breathe. The gulls, the twin clocks, the Seine flowing under the timeless arches of Pont Royal. The Paris inside the old city walls is another world. Even the weather seems kinder. The rain has stopped, and a patch of blue is breaking through the clouds. As I walk through the Saint-Thomas-d'Aquin quarter, there's a new air in me. I'm no longer the girl from the suburbs. I'm Parisian. The storm has washed the city clean. The buildings in Rue de Bellechasse are shining like freshly minted coins.

Let's do this!

Workdays seem less of a struggle in the nice parts of the city. Especially when they start with my favourite patient.

I ring the buzzer and take the lift to the fifth floor.

'Hello, Angélique. How are you this morning?'

It's my fourth visit to Stella Petrenko's flat, and it's always a highlight of the day. We have our little routine. I change her dressing, she pours me an orange-flavoured black tea, then we chat for five minutes next to her imposing silver samovar. I like her flat – the way it's decorated, the sweeping view over the rooftops, the original waxed parquet. She's never short on things to say. The old ballerina has a sharp mind and a sense of humour to match. She passes on book and film recommendations, tells me glittering anecdotes about her career. And for a moment, I feel like I'm finally *where I'm meant to be*. I tell myself that I too could be part of this world where life is filled with possibility. Break free of my stultifying routine. Escape the narrow horizon of the suburbs.

I've always tried to pull myself up: by studying, by networking, by dating, seduction, manipulation. I know how to be a chameleon. For a long time, I truly believed that one day, I'd jump the invisible barrier that's kept me on the wrong side of the tracks. But over the years and the disappointments they've dealt me, that conviction has faded. I've learnt my strengths and weaknesses. I know there are two forces inside me. The tussle between angel and devil. On good days, I can play the game like a pro, bottle up my worries, frustrations and anger, channel the chaos raging in my mind. On those days, people can find me charming, thoughtful, irresistible. I'm sure that's what Stella Petrenko's thinking right now.

'Did you hear that?' she asks, suddenly replacing her cup on the table.

An alarming crash has just come from upstairs. Like someone knocking over a heavy dresser full of crockery. Then silence.

'It must have come from Marco's flat,' Stella says. 'It isn't like him, he's usually quiet as a mouse.'

'Maybe we should go up to investigate.'

She nods. I follow her onto the landing. As the lift doesn't go higher than the fifth floor, we take the stairs together.

'Who is Marco, anyway?'

'Marco Sabatini. He's a young Italian painter. A bit odd, but very sweet. He came to ask me for some paracetamol yesterday. He was coughing his lungs up – he looked awful. I suggested calling an emergency doctor, but he didn't want to.'

I rap repeatedly on the door.

'Mr Sabatini?'

No answer.

'Are you there, Mr Sabatini?'

I try the handle, but the door's locked.

'Will the caretaker have a spare set of keys?'

'I'm sure she does,' Stella replies. 'But she's on holiday . . .'

I scan around.

'What's through there?'

'The old service stairs.'

I push open the metal door to reveal a narrow stairwell with a ladder leading up to a smoke vent. For all my faults, I have my uses. I know how to keep a cool head in a crisis. I climb up the ladder, tilt open the window and hoist myself out.

'Careful, it's not safe up there!' Stella cries.

Her voice is distorted by the echo, drowned out by the wind. As I crouch on the roof, it's like I've entered a different world. The view is breathtaking. A dizzying sea of slate and zinc. I stand up halfway, trying to keep steady. The wind's so strong it takes me a moment to find my footing and my bearings. Shielding my eyes against the glare, I spot a row of dormer windows that must lead into Sabatini's flat. As I crawl along the guttering, a sudden gust almost blows me off balance. I'm shaking, giddy with fear. A whoop of nervous laughter bursts from my lips. I like out-of-the-ordinary moments like this, moments that make you feel today won't be any old day. One of the windows is wide open. Just a few yards more, and I manage to slip through the gap without breaking my neck.

4

I let out a sigh of relief as I land in the flat. The place is incredible. All the old servants' rooms on the sixth floor have been knocked through to create a vast artist's studio, which must span at least 500 square feet. The whole floor is under the eaves, with a series of skylights illuminating the space.

Despite the breeze from the windows, a powerful smell of turpentine hangs in the air. As I scan the room, I see Marco Sabatini's body sprawled on the parquet between two trestles. Around him are a jumble of paint pots and broken glass jars, and a workbench that he must have dragged with him as he fell.

I pull from my pocket the surgical mask I'd taken off before scaling the roof.

'Mr Sabatini, can you hear me?' I ask, crouching next to him. 'How are you feeling?'

He's barely thirty. His shoulder-length hair is plastered with sweat, his chin overrun with stubble. Like an angel who's just shot up on heroin.

I lean over him and press my hand to his forehead. It's burning. He tries to mutter something, but he's so breathless his voice is inaudible.

'I'm a nurse. We're going to take care of you.'

I stand up to unlock the front door.

'Your neighbour's in a bad way, Stella. Could you grab my bag? I left it in your flat.'

'Of course.'

I return to my patient. He's wearing a paint-spattered white linen shirt, with the sleeves rolled up to reveal a collection of tattoos – the five-point star of the Red Brigades, a dove of peace, a raised fist, a bloodied combat knife, '*Wish You Were Here*' in English, an anti-capitalist quote proclaiming '*the paradise of the rich is made out of the hell of the poor*'.

'Have you been vaccinated against Covid, Mr Sabatini?'

From the middle finger he jabs in my direction, I'm guessing not.

He's curled in the foetal position. His left hand is clenched to his chest, and his pyjama bottoms are streaked with diarrhoea. He's coughing so hard he's almost suffocating. As Stella returns with my bag, I ask her not to come in.

'There's every chance he's contagious.'

I slide the oximeter onto Sabatini's index finger. As I feared, his blood oxygen level is below 90 percent, requiring urgent hospitalisation.

I phone the emergency switchboard and explain why I'm calling. The minion at the other end takes an eternity to set up a file on his PC. Classic summer chaos in the French health service. I tell him I'm a nurse and that my patient is in respiratory distress. As the little shit is getting above his station, I press him to transfer the call to a medical specialist. The physician agrees with my diagnosis – a probable case of critical Covid – and immediately dispatches an ambulance unit.

Ten minutes later, a doctor, nurse and paramedic arrive on the sixth floor. In a frenzy of gloves, gowns and goggles, they rush to give Sabatini first aid. I offer my assistance, but the three men prefer to keep things among themselves. In the end, they decide to stretcher out the painter and continue treatment in the ambulance.

I remain alone for a moment in the empty flat. There are three canvases propped on easels. Strange portraits each showing the same, mercury-eyed figure set against different backgrounds. Sabatini has painted himself. A Renaissance Italian prince. Lorenzo the Magnificent, living-dead-style.

The place has me fascinated and freaked all at once. I lock the door behind me, intending to return the keys, but when

I reach the ground floor, I realise they're too big to post through the caretaker's pigeonhole.

'Ah, Angélique! We need you!'

I turn to see the nurse calling to me from the pavement. He's a weird-looking specimen – shaven head, one prosthetic eye that's buried deep in its socket, albino eyebrows.

'You're still here?' I ask, registering the double-parked ambulance. 'How's the patient?'

'Not good. We've intubated and ventilated him.'

He tilts his chin at the doctor, who's glued to his phone a little further down the street.

'The doc's trying to find him an ICU bed, but it's touch-and-go. It's always a nightmare in the holidays.'

'Tell me about it.'

'I'm Esteban, by the way.'

I nod back. His fucked-up appearance made me clock him as soon as he arrived. Not the sharpest tool in the box, but kind of poignant. He's clutching the tablet on which he's meant to be filling out the ambulance report.

'The doc asked me to help him with this, but I'm struggling. Do you know the patient's name?'

'Marco Sabatini.'

'How do you spell it?'

'Start typing it into the search box – the system will auto-fill the rest.'

'Could you talk me through it?'

I scan the screen and help him to complete a few sections of the form. One of the fields asks the patient to nominate an 'Emergency contact'. Without giving it much thought, I leave my own name: 'Angélique Charvet, friend.'

6

A BIT MAD

1

8 p.m.

My last visit is done: a shot of anticoagulant to a cranky old bastard in Rue d'Assas. I don't know where the day has gone. I've drawn a veil over my negative thoughts: the pregnancy test, the impending abortion, Corentin Lelièvre's idiot face. It's a lovely evening. The sky is pink, full of promise. I've zero inclination to cram inside a skanky commuter train back to Aulnay. Resolved to make the most of a few more hours in Paris, I head back up Boulevard Raspail with my hands in my cagoule pockets. And that's when I remember I haven't returned the keys to Marco Sabatini's flat.

As Rue de Bellechasse is just up the road, I go back with the intention of leaving the keys with Stella Petrenko. I punch in both door codes to enter the building, then take the lift to the fifth floor. My finger is all set to press the bell. Then I hesitate. The urge seems to hit me from nowhere. To see the studio again. Alone. I tiptoe up to the sixth floor, slot the key in the lock and find myself nose-to-nose with Sabatini's trio of portraits.

'All right, guys? Hope I haven't spoilt the wake?'

The three pairs of silvery eyes stare straight through me. The floorboards creak under my footsteps, the stench of turpentine bringing back memories of my grandpa's joinery workshop.

I lift the blinds to let some light in. With its the vast proportions and exposed beams, the loft really is majestic. Scale aside, though, the place is austere, almost entirely devoted to the act of creation. Trestles and easels have replaced furniture, and the parquet is a constellation of coloured splotches. Everywhere I turn there are paint pots, palettes and cloths, splayed sketchpads and jars of motley-sized brushes.

I nose around, examining the contents of the fridge, cupboards and drawers like I own the place. Realising I'm hungry, I snaffle a few Jaffa Cakes, a Gala apple and an out-of-date yogurt. In the bathroom, I hit on the drugs stash that the ambulance-team doctor must have unearthed before me. Sabatini's no small-time dabbler – coke, ecstasy pills, a tube of OxyContin, snap bags of Spice. I eye them in distaste. I've always been careful to distance myself from that world. The chaos in my head doesn't need any help with turning my life to carnage. All the same, I can't resist a couple of shots from the bottle of honey vodka I find in the freezer.

Under a storage unit, I spot Sabatini's phone. It must have slid under there when he collapsed this morning. Clearly, he tried to call for help himself before he blacked out. Suddenly a ringtone sounds. Not from the painter's phone, but from my own.

'Angélique Charvet?'

'Speaking.'

'I'm calling from the Intensive Care Unit at Pompidou Hospital. We've got your boyfriend with us, Mr Marco Sabatini.'

'Sorry?'

I'm thrown for a moment. Then I put two and two together. The ambulance report has been transferred to the hospital, and the nurse thinks I'm her patient's partner. His *girlfriend*, rather than his *friend*.

The news isn't good. As I'd assumed, the virus has spread to his lungs, leaving them no choice but to put him in a medically induced coma. From what the nurse tells me, I gather that the hospital is keen for information about their Italian charge's treatment history. She asks me if he's already registered with a doctor or health centre. Before hanging up, I promise I'll do my best to find out.

2

Taking the honey vodka with me, I head out to the balcony and flop onto the clapped-out rattan rocking chair the painter has commandeered as a sun lounger. The pastel tones of the sky have taken on the same orangey glow as my bottle of Krupnik.

The device that I've salvaged from the floor is an ancient iPhone with a broken screen. The splinters of glass look as if they might come loose and stab me at any minute, but the thing still works and isn't password-protected. Sabatini is patently not a phone addict. On first inspection, there's nothing of interest. The painter uses it for two purposes: for placing orders with his dealer, and for exchanging hundreds of text messages with his mother, who goes by the name of Bianca.

His messages are sent in flurries, during moments of crisis. Periods in which the terrified *bambino* is plagued by nightmarish visions, repeatedly claiming that 'the army of the dead' are coming for him. Then, as soon as calm returns to Marco's life, their exchanges fall silent – sometimes for months on end. From the evidence on the screen, mother and son haven't spoken since last Christmas. As I scroll further back, I can tell the Italian has his *mamma* wrapped around his little finger, assuring her that his addiction problems are behind him. And she's gullible enough to believe him.

Or, more plausibly, maybe she prefers to turn a blind eye?

Reading through the thread, it's also obvious they don't see each other often. Bianca Sabatini lives between Turin and Venice and travels frequently, flitting around the US, Asia and various European capitals. A company name repeatedly crops up: AcquaAlta. I'm vaguely familiar with the clothing brand, having seen their stuff on Instagram and from passing the shop in Avenue Montaigne. A luxury boutique, specialising in cashmere that can easily cost half my salary.

Back on my own phone, I run a Google search for 'Sabatini family' and 'AcquaAlta'. I need to know more. The results are enlightening – and intriguing: Marco Sabatini is the heir of an eminent Italian dynasty. As I click through the links, the story of the empire gradually comes into focus.

Originally from Piedmont, the Sabatini family began working in the cloth and wool trade in the mid-nineteenth century. The manufacturing business AcquaAlta was established at the end of the First World War, initially with a string of spinning mills in northern Italy, before expanding its operations in the twenties to supply high-quality textiles to some of the biggest fashion houses of the day – including French giants Paul Poiret, Lanvin, Vionnet and Chanel.

During the post-Second World War boom years, the company developed its international arm by exporting to Asia and the US, but underwent a change of direction in the nineties when Lisandro Sabatini – Marco's father, aka *l'Ingegnere* ('the Engineer') – took the reins. His upscaling strategy focused on the production of a very fine wool obtained from chilihueques, an extremely rare species of llama found only in the Chilean mountains. After the fall of Pinochet, AcquaAlta struck deals with successive Chilean governments to expand the breeding of the animal, which was at that point on the brink of extinction.

Soon, major luxury brands were scrambling to get their hands on the wool, which commanded a premium price for being finer than cashmere and reportedly one of the most comfortable wools to wear. As the final stage in its rebrand, AcquaAlta launched its own clothing line, sold through a network of luxury stores – a move that brought runaway economic success and sealed the company's status as a tasty going concern.

In recent years, I read that LVMH, Kering and Richemont have all made bids to acquire the brand, sometimes dubbed 'the Italian Hermès'. But the Sabatini family has repeatedly spurned the advances of the big players. In his rare public statements, *l'Ingegnere* has insisted at every turn that AcquaAlta will remain an authentic family business, and will always resist 'the soulless clutches of global corporations'.

3

After the economics lesson, it's time to hit the gossip magazines. I discover that in the early 2000s, *Oggi* and *Gente* – Italy's answer to *Paris Match* – published a series of photo reports on the Sabatini family. Taken when Marco and his twin sister, Livia, were young teenagers, the images project a vision of family bliss – Riva yacht cruises on Lake Como, skiing trips in Cortina d'Ampezzo, holidays at their villa on the Cap d'Antibes. But aged just nineteen, Livia was killed in a hiking accident in the Dolomites. After that, Marco spiralled off the rails, lurching from heroin addiction to anti-capitalist rebellion and all manner of misdemeanours in between. A 2015 article in the *Corriere della Sera* summed up his fall from grace:

Marco Sabatini, *enfant terrible* of the AcquaAlta empire, rushed to hospital after overdose

The son of Lisandro Sabatini, the principal shareholder of the AcquaAlta group, was recovered unconscious yesterday morning from a squat in Milan's Quarto Oggiaro district. The alarm was raised by a fellow drug addict, who claimed that *l'Ingegnere*'s son had taken the equivalent of five grams of cocaine after injecting himself with heroin. Marco Sabatini was rushed to Niguarda Hospital, though he is reported to be out of immediate danger.

A graduate of the Brera Fine Arts Academy, the twenty-five-year-old became the sole heir of the Sabatini dynasty on the death of his sister, Livia, but has repeat-edly stated that he wants no role in the company. While at university, he ran a student website inspired by anti-liberal and environmentalist politics, on which he wrote that: *Capitalism is the root of all society's problems. It's fundamentally incompatible with our survival as a human species. Ultimately it will destroy itself, but we can't just sit back and wait for that to happen. The eradication of the bourgeoisie must begin now, and violence is the only way to achieve this.*

By the time I look up from my phone screen, darkness has fallen. The studio is bathed in an inky bluish glow. Across the street, a teenager in a headset is playing on a giant screen. Further away, I can hear ripples of voices – the muted rev-elry of Paris in August, three-quarters empty and, for a few weeks, restored to a country village atmosphere. I've finished the bottle of vodka. Tipsily, I shut my eyes for a moment. It's a weird sensation. Despite my whirring head, I feel incred-ibly lucid.

I've always found night a soothing time. My frustrations are less acute, my thoughts crisper, more constructive. But even then, I can't stop the same niggling misery washing back over me. The sense that life's passing me by. That I'm a stranger in my own story. A spectator unable to write my own score. The sense of rusting away on the sidings with the trains bound for nowhere. The belief that I deserve better, as if God cocked up when dealing the cards that allow us to play out our lives.

'*How do all these other people get everything right?*' the old song asks. How does everyone else succeed, when I can't even get a foothold in the world before it spins away from me? I'm out of step, mired on a parallel track that's stuck on repeat. Over the years, I've lost myself. Even I don't know who I am anymore. Nor what I'm truly looking *for*.

A bit mad.

Sooner or later, the words always come back to bite me.

You're a bit mad, Angélique.

From my mother. From women who were once my friends. From the handful of men who've fallen in and out in my life.

A bit mad, my girl.

A bit mad for being repulsed by the mediocrity around me and feeling trapped by it. A bit mad for thinking that life has a different texture on the other side of the tracks. A bit mad for not swallowing the fantasy that it's the simple pleasures that are the essence of happiness. A bit mad for wanting to run away, for telling myself that another life is possible. A bit mad for always preferring 'the folly of the passions to the wisdom of indifference'. A bit mad for dreaming of better than the dead-beat losers who toss out chat-up lines from behind a screen while playing online poker and wanking off on Pornhub.

4

I snap open my eyes. An idea has flashed into my mind. One that's 'a bit mad', as it happens. I reach for Marco's phone again and dial the number . . . for his mother. The call takes forever to connect. I can feel myself shaking. I'm on the brink of hanging up. Then I recognise the North American call tone, and a voice answers:

'*Marco, mi amore, va bene?*'

'Hello, Mrs Sabatini, please forgive me for ringing from your son's phone, but—'

'Who are you?' she asks, this time in French.

'My name's Angélique Charvet. I wanted to let you know that Marco's been taken ill.'

'*O Dio mio!* Is it serious? Where is he?'

'In Georges Pompidou Hospital.'

I take the time to explain the situation. I can hear her distress at the other end of the line, yet also her determination not to crumble or allow her emotions to stop her thinking clearly.

'I'm in New York,' she tells me. 'It's 3 p.m. here. I'll try to catch a plane to Paris this evening. Thank you for letting me know.'

'Don't mention it.'

'Do you have the number for the hospital?'

I relay it to her, then offer: 'Would you like me to meet you at the airport?'

'Erm . . . why?'

'That way, we could go straight to the hospital, to see Marco together.'

I leave a very long pause before continuing.

'I suspected as much. Marco hasn't told you about me, has he?'

'I . . . I don't think so, no.'

'I'm Angélique, his girlfriend.'

7

THE REPLACEMENT

1

Six days later
4 September 2021
Avenue Montaigne

In the late Paris summer, the courtyard of the Plaza Athénée was the beating heart of the palace. An oasis of cool and calm away from the roar of the traffic. The walls of the building were twined in ivy and vines from top to bottom, the balconies spilling with flowering geraniums as red as the parasols.

A taste of true life as I'd imagined it. On the other side of the tracks, everything was brighter, stronger, more exhilarating. At last, I was the star of a film in which I had the lead role. A film where the set wasn't made from cardboard, and the actors playing opposite me were from the Juilliard School rather than the Villeneuve-les-Deux-Verges community theatre group.

Since Bianca Sabatini's arrival in France, it was there, on the hotel's restaurant terrace, that we'd taken to meeting each morning – just the two of us, over a light breakfast. Her husband, *l'Ingegnere*, had stayed in Milan to look after the family's empire. He'd initially tried to have his son transferred to the American Hospital in Neuilly, but had backed down after being assured of the first-class care at the Pompidou.

Bianca adored me. Because I knew how to comfort her. Because she was convinced of my love for her *bambino*. And because I had a wonderful story to tell.

I'd met Marco two years earlier, on Quai Voltaire. He was heading out of the Sennelier shop after stocking up on paint supplies, and I was leaving a patient's flat after a blood test. After almost knocking each other flying, we'd got chatting and had hit it off immediately. Marco had invited me back to his studio, then out for dinner at Septime. At the time, he'd unfortunately started using again, but as love works miracles, I'd helped him to kick the habit and we'd moved in together. I'd encouraged him to carry on with his portrait series and to show the paintings to the art dealer, Bernard Benedick. In the evenings, we liked to order prawn curry from Le Petit Cambodge and watch Netflix series. On Sundays, we went running in the Jardin du Luxembourg and for bike rides along the Canal de l'Ourcq, and occasionally we'd spend a weekend by the seaside at my mum's house in Trouville. For our next holiday, Marco had promised to take me to see the Northern Lights in Iceland. A heart-warming pair of loved-up city slickers, living the bohemian dream in Hidalgo's Paris.

In Bianca's eyes, I was the guardian angel she'd always hoped for, sent from above to set her son back on the right path. The steadying force who'd managed to build a safe cocoon for the apple of her eye. She found me reassuring – I wasn't a grasping footballer's wife, a brassy bimbo or a gold-digging hussy from the clubs along the Champs-Élysées. I was a sweet little nurse, an everyday hero who'd battled 'on the front line' against Covid. I was selfless, always putting other people first. I'd been a volunteer at the Doctors of the World emergency clinic in Plaine-Saint-Denis (that much was true, even if it hadn't lasted long). My parents were teachers. I could hold a conversation about Renaissance painting, I'd seen films by Antonioni and Nanni Moretti and I knew who Mario Draghi and Matteo Renzi were. A nice ordinary girl, just as a rich person would imagine her.

And however much Bianca loved me, I have to admit it was mutual. The woman fascinated me. With her sincere kindness, her effortless refinement. Even in the face of crisis, she was a model of patrician dignity. A youthful sixty, with harmonious features and barely a hint of grey in her blonde chignon. Her clothes exuded unassuming elegance and, wherever she sat, a timely beam of sunlight would always appear to seal her look of a regal Madonna.

She spoke perfect French, but would often burst into Italian in the heat of the moment. She liked talking about her philanthropy with the flagship AcquaAlta Foundation, which supported education, the arts and the fight against poverty through the development of microcredit. The Foundation had offices in Manhattan and Turin and provided millions of euros in aid.

But her favourite subject, of course, was her dear Marco, about whom she worried so much. Every time we spoke, she fleshed out the portrait of the prodigal son a bit more. For me, it was a classic story of a screwed-up rich kid. For her, it was the parable of a 'bright, brilliant and sensitive boy' who had '*molto sofferto*' ('suffered deeply').

'Maybe I've already told you this, *Angelica,* but it was his sister's death that changed everything. Livia and Marco were incredibly close, practically inseparable. The invincible duo. When Livia left us, there's no doubt Marco wanted to join her. *Inconsciamente.* Almost without realising it, he set about destroying his life, challenging our authority, refusing to work in the family business and spouting left-wing views.'

'To get his father's *attenzione*?' I prompted, mobilising the dregs of my sixth-form Italian.

'*Probabilmente!* There's every chance! But Lisandro had no time for it. He loves his son, but not as much as AcquaAlta, the legacy his family has built over six generations.'

'Did your husband want Livia to take over the business?'

'*Sì.* Marco has always been a gentle soul, too much of an artist for Lisandro's liking. He's never lived up to the hopes his father had for him. That's why they stopped talking nine years ago. My husband even cut off his allowance, although he's probably guessed that I was the one who paid for the studio in Rue de Bellechasse and . . .'

Bianca's sentence was left hanging, interrupted by the trill of her phone. As soon as she picked up, I could tell from her face it was the hospital.

For the first time, it was good news about Marco. His secondary lung infection was abating, his general condition was improving and the medical team thought he might start breathing by himself again. Bianca's expression lit up. In her excitement, she squeezed my forearm and put the phone on loudspeaker so that we could share in the rapturous moment.

'We've started reducing his medication and we're going to lower the sedation too,' the doctor announced.

'*È una notizia eccezionale!* What wonderful news! *Una grande speranza!*'

'We'll see how your son responds, but it will take a while for him to come round. We'd like you both to be there when he wakes up – Miss Charvet and yourself. The process is often easier when there are familiar faces. Patients feel less disorientated.'

2

Bianca wanted to make for the Pompidou immediately, but thankfully the doctor dissuaded her. Marco's return to consciousness would be very gradual, taking at least a day or two. We were better saving our energy for the next day, when our presence would be more useful. In her elation, Bianca couldn't entertain sitting around doing nothing. While we waited it out, she resolved to spend the afternoon decking out Marco's flat, anxious that her *bambino* should have a snug nest in which to continue his recovery.

The loft was the weak link in my plan. Before Bianca's first visit to Rue de Bellechasse, I'd hastily brought over a few possessions to bolster the illusion of my life with her son, but I could tell it wasn't what she'd been expecting. I'd had to cobble together an explanation: Marco and I divided our time between my flat and his studio.

After a trip to the homeware stores on Boulevard Saint-Germain, we spent the rest of the day cleaning and rejigging the layout of the studio. Bianca and her credit card had a magic touch. On discovering their client's identity, the staff in Knoll offered her various items of display furniture – a Saarinen table, Chandigarh chairs, an Eames lounge chair with matching ottoman and a shaggy cream rug – and arranged for them to be delivered that afternoon. By the time we'd finished, the loft could have graced the cover of *Architectural Digest*.

I felt feverish. A ruthless storm was about to rip through my carefully constructed house of cards. Yet I also sensed in me an uncharted strength. A fire that, instead of consuming me, held out new, infinite possibilities. I liked the story I'd served up to Bianca. I liked my new life. Even if it was built on a lie, couldn't reality be adjusted to match the fiction I'd created? When the fairy godmothers visited my crib, they might not have stopped long, but they did give me a dose of gumption and that seed of madness which, in that moment, urged me to risk whatever it took.

That evening, before we parted, Bianca and I fell into each other's arms. I accompanied her down to her cab, then she clasped me to her again, kissing my cheeks and ruffling my hair, so sure that we were on the eve of brighter days to come. *Grazie Angelica, grazie figlia mia.* Thank you, daughter of mine.

Even once she was inside the car, the Italian wound down her window to keep talking to me. Marco's life was going to restart on the right track. In the end, the ordeal would prove to be a blessing. *I momenti belli e quelli difficili, non durano per sempre.* Neither the good times nor the bad last forever.

At last the driver started the engine. I reciprocated Bianca's goodbye with equally animated waving. Once the taxi was out of sight, I stayed on the pavement for almost a minute, hit by a yawning sense of emptiness. Then I went back up to the flat for my bag.

As usual, I was worried I might bump into the caretaker, who was now back from her holidays. But the main lodge was in the other building and, from the little I'd seen of the woman – I'd only passed her once and she'd totally blanked me – she took a pretty limited view of her responsibilities.

I closed the door silently behind me and continued into the studio. As I did so, I saw the newly installed, beige leather Eames spin on its axle. I let out a little cry of surprise.

There, sitting cross-legged in the lounge chair, was Stella Petrenko, watching me with a thin smile on her lips.

3

'You think I haven't worked out your little game?' the former ballerina spat at me.

'It's not polite to listen at doors, Ms Petrenko.'

I tried not to show my unease, but that evening, with her turban, dark felt boots and the huge black shawl swathing her body, the dancer scared me.

'Tricking Mrs Sabatini into believing you're Marco's fiancée – that's your plan, is it?'

'I don't think that's any of your business.'

'Oh, but it is. I'm very fond of Marco.'

Her face had contorted beyond recognition. There was no longer a trace of warmth or friendliness. Just a fixed smile that gave her the look of a pantomime witch.

'Are you familiar with the concept of *Schadenfreude*, Angélique?'

'Enlighten me.'

'It's a German word for the kick you get from seeing other people's misery.'

With a flick of the hand the dancer produced a cigarette, which she lit with a strange pearl-encrusted lighter.

'You know, the kind of guilty pleasure you feel when younger, prettier, richer, brighter women get a good slap in the face.'

'It's not enough to be happy: you need other people to be miserable. Is that it?'

'Got it in one.'

She drew in a long puff of smoke before continuing.

'When the wrinkles around your eyes get deeper, when you're incapable of shifting those extra pounds, when your breasts shrivel and your chin starts to sag as if it wants to pack its bags, when men stop clocking you in the street . . .'

She broke off to take another drag.

'. . . All that comes quickly, trust me, and it's brutal. And when it does – when you see that your best years are behind you, that life will never have the same thrill again – you become bitter and mean. And one morning, you realise that your last remaining joy is watching other people suffer.'

'Not very edifying, is it?'

'True, but that's how it goes. You don't feel compassion or pity anymore. Instead, you get a perverse buzz. It's a comfort, knowing you're not the only one whose life is shit.'

'Why are you telling me this?'

'Because I saw through you from day one. I never swallowed your butter-wouldn't-melt act. And you know what? I think you're *like me*, stewing in anger and resentment. And now, you're thinking you might have found a way out of your crappy little life, your ticket to playing with the big fish.'

'But why are *you* so angry?'

Stella Petrenko gave a sour laugh.

'Because I was in the spotlight and now I'm not. Once you've had a taste of that life, everything else pales in comparison. Leaving the stage is awful. Performers aren't meant to live in the shadows.'

As though mirroring her venomous words, her face suddenly reminded me of Gloria Swanson in *Sunset Boulevard* – haggard skin, mascara-caked eyelashes, lips frothing with saliva, high, crescent-moon brows.

'I'm going to have a word with Mrs Sabatini,' she threatened. 'And I tell you this: she'll be very cross about your little fib. If there's one thing a mother *hates*, it's having someone take advantage of her son.'

'Let's not get ahead of ourselves, Ms Petrenko. I'm sure we can reach an understanding.'

'I don't see how.'

From the canvas bag I'd left on the coffee table, I retrieved a thick, white envelope and handed it to her.

The former dancer opened it, then sat gaping for a moment at the wads of fifty-euro notes. She began counting them: one, two, three, five, nine, ten . . .

'Ten thousand euros. That's a fair compromise, don't you think?'

She weighed up the notes with both hands, eyeing them like precious jewels, practically sniffing them.

'Where did you get this kind of cash?' she asked, realising she'd underestimated me.

She looked up, scanning the flat. Then her eyes lit up, and she cracked out laughing.

'You sold the paintings, didn't you? You've already sold Marco's three portraits, you little bitch!'

8

THE POINT OF NO RETURN

1

After Stella Petrenko had left, I remained alone in the flat for a long time, leaning on my elbows over the balcony rail with all the lights out.

The stench of paint and glue was making my head swim. So, this evening would be the moment of truth. I couldn't kid myself: the challenge was steeper than I'd thought. It had also come sooner than I'd bargained for. But if I gave in to panic, everything would come crashing down. At all costs, I had to keep up the adrenaline and the positive momentum of the past few days. The untapped powers that I'd felt stirring in me and the sense of possibility they brought. I needed to solve each problem in turn. Spring into action. *Now.*

I took the stairs down to the street. The night was hot and close. I had no desire to return to the furnace of the metro. There was a self-service bike station a few streets away, in Rue Casimir Périer. At first glance, there was a wide selection available – blue electric models and classic green ones – except that, as usual, none of them were working. The council might have been all for 'soft mobility', but in practice

their 'peaceful city' was just a green-lobby-cowed waste-
land where everything was falling to bits. The flop of the
bike scheme was a classic example – punctured tyres, stolen
wheels, dead batteries, broken chains. In the end, I took a
basic model with a buckled wheel. The brakes screeched like
hell and one of the pedals was falling off, but it was that or
nothing.

Come on, girl. Time to roll.

The fresh air was a relief, the exertion helping to calm
my nerves a little. After turning onto Rue de l'Université,
I wove up Rue de Solférino to the Seine. From there, I just
had to continue west along the riverbank. The quayside was
swarming with people. It was Saturday evening, and a car-
nival atmosphere reigned as Parisians ate, drank and danced
out the last of summer against a backdrop of the Eiffel Tower
and Pont Mirabeau. Alcohol, music and drugs to banish the
interminable pandemic, mask-wearing, tests and threats of a
return to lockdown.

After passing Parc André Citroën, I returned my bike to
the station in Place du Moulin-de-Javel and headed for the
hospital building.

2

Pompidou Hospital is a pile of blocks that looks like it's been
built from giant Lego by a not-very-gifted child. Resting
my bag on a bus-stop bench, I pull out my nurse's uniform
– button-up tunic and elasticated-waist trousers – and slip it
over my jeans and T-shirt.

For all the building's faults, the glass roof over the atrium still works its charm every time. It's 10 p.m. With the A&E entrance located on the other side of the building, in Rue Delbarre, the main hospital is fairly quiet. In the other-worldly blue glow coming through the skylights, the place almost has the feel of a spaceship.

Having accompanied Bianca here every day for the past week, I've had time to get my bearings and know the layout of the lobby by heart. Although there are night security guards on duty, they're too bound up with policing the Covid regulations. The CCTV cameras don't faze me either. There's no point keeping my head down. I just have to look like an everyday nurse, bustling off to start my shift or responding to a call for backup.

I waver for a second, unsure whether to go any further. My plan hinges on a sequence of variables that aren't all within my control. But I also know that nothing will change if I don't take the gamble. I've spent twenty years waiting for this. Twenty years of watching out for a window of opportunity. I've always believed that in life, we get one shot at changing the course of our fate. The Ancient Greeks called it *kairos*: the magic moment that can flip everything on its head. The blink of an eye in which we need to *act*, before the chance slips from our grasp forever.

Now.

Before the window closes again.

I press the button to call the lift, select the first floor. Every inch of me is trembling. There's still time to turn back. It's as if every decision I've made up to now, good or bad, has served only to lead me here. To this crossroads that will determine the second chapter of my life, at which I've everything to gain and everything to lose.

The doors open onto the corridors of the ICU.

I'm assaulted by the smell of disinfectant and poorly reheated food, giving me an urge to gag that reminds me of the cluster of cells complicating my plan. As though guided by an invisible force, I continue through the maze of metal trolleys, stretchers and plastic chairs until I reach Sabatini's room. Thanks to Daddy's string-pulling, the heir has a private suite. I need to be quick. A doctor, nurse or care assistant could burst in at any second. I observe my 'fiancé' lying on his back, his eyes taped shut with thin plasters. With his beard and long hair, there's a Jesus-like look about him, with his tangle of drips and catheters for a crown of thorns. In steady waves, the monitor tracks his vital signs – heart and respiratory rate, blood pressure, oxygen saturation – the twinkling testament to my beloved's return to health.

3

If one day I'm called to stand trial, I won't be able to claim my actions weren't premediated. I've done my homework, mulling the problem over and over, researching everything I could. I even phoned a nurse friend who works in ICU, trying to pass it off as a casual enquiry. My original thought was a rapid shot of potassium chloride – a standard 5g KCl syringe, normally administered over several hours to treat hypokalaemia, delivered in one fell swoop. By injecting the whole thing at once, straight into his veins, the plasma concentration would be enough to trigger bradycardia and asystole. The rub: potassium is routinely measured in electrolyte tests, so would show up on the post-mortem. Goodbye to that idea, then.

My chest feels like it's caught in a vice. I swallow hard and take a deep breath. Will the plan I've hatched stand up to scrutiny? And do I truly have the guts to go through with it?

I pull a first-aid pouch from my rucksack. Inside, there's a syringe protected by a safety cap. Calcium works differently to potassium. A rapid shot of six or seven grams of calcium chloride will send the heart into a frenzy, leading to ventricular tachycardia and fibrillation until it stops beating altogether. The plus: calcium isn't part of a standard electrolyte test. They won't find it unless they actively *look for it*.

Do I dare?

I silence the voice telling me I'm done for. Instead, I tell myself it's now or never, that I know exactly what I'm doing. And that I take full responsibility. The only way to a fresh start is to break with what's gone before.

I position the needle.

Then I let out a yelp.

Fuck!

Sabatini has just opened his eyes through the plasters! He grabs my arm with all his pathetic might and stares at me half-dazed, half-terrified. Managing to stop myself shouting, I find the courage to hold his gaze. And I push the plunger.

I know that there'll be a *before* and an *after*.

That I've crossed a point of no return.

But that's the price I had to pay to reclaim my life.

9

ONE OF THE FAMILY

Jean Renoir

1

Death of Marco Sabatini, taken by Covid-19
La Stampa – in association with AFP

The painter Marco Sabatini, the son Lisandro and Bianca Sabatini, has died in Paris following complications linked to Covid-19.

Having spent several days in the intensive care unit at Georges Pompidou European Hospital, the young artist suffered a rapid deterioration in his condition on Saturday night.

Despite becoming the sole heir of the AcquaAlta luxury clothing group in 2009, following the death of his sister Livia, Marco Sabatini resolutely kept his distance from the family business and had been living in Paris for several years. His work has been on show at the prestigious Bernard Benedick gallery since 2019.

'Our son Marco has gone to join his sister Livia,' his parents wrote in a statement. 'Despite the tireless care and commitment of the medical staff, and his own courageous struggle against the illness, Marco didn't have the strength to win the battle.'

Following in family tradition, Marco Sabatini will be buried in Tortona (Piedmont), the symbolic seat of the dynasty for the past two hundred years.

He was 31 years old.

2

6 September 2021

Lisandro Sabatini has invited me to meet him in Chez Luca, a classy trattoria in Rue du Boccador with dark wood panelling, glossy almond-green walls and a red-and-white chequered floor. It's only ten in the morning, but they've opened especially for him.

The rain is back, smothering Paris under a grim blanket of humidity that's only compounded by the dim lighting of the restaurant. *L'Ingegnere* is waiting on a black leather banquette along the back wall, behind a small, pearly-grey marble table. With his staidly suave appearance and slick tailoring, the businessman matches the photos I've seen of him online. Tall, trim frame, close-fitting, wide-lapelled suit, Oxford brogues, F.P. Journe Chronomètre à Résonance watch sported over his shirt cuff like Gianni Agnelli.

With a hand he beckons me to take the seat opposite him.

He studies me for a few seconds, but not in a way that makes me uncomfortable.

'I'd like to have met under different circumstances, Angélique, but such is life. Bianca's told me what a support you've been to her these past few days, and I'm grateful to you.'

I nod, trying to hold my nerve, focusing on the wall behind him with its black-and-white stills of barren Puglian and Sicilian landscapes.

Sabatini continues in a grim tone.

'I can't say I'm surprised by how things have turned out. I've spent a long time expecting to receive news of my son's death, sooner or later. My money would have been on an overdose, or suicide, or a knife attack by a dealer. But no, in the end, it was that bastard Covid . . .'

He pulls from his pocket a picture of Marco and his sister in all their glorious innocence. Beaming ten-year-olds, having the time of their life in a multicoloured ball pit. The boundless joys of childhood.

'Marco and I might not have spoken for years, but I never forgot all the happy times we shared when he was a boy.'

At my silence, Lisandro grows more impassioned.

'Marco must have told you the most awful things about me, but none of it's true. Despite my work commitments, I wasn't a distant father, or an absent one. I took him and his sister to school every morning. I helped them with their homework every afternoon, then came back in the evening to read them a story before returning to the office. Bianca and I didn't raise our kids like royalty, we—'

'Marco never said anything awful about you,' I cut in. 'He

just wished you'd allowed him to choose his own path in life.'

'His own path in life? But since when did any of us get a choice? Did *you*?'

Sabatini loosens the knot of his tie.

'Let's be honest. Marco spent his time painting zombies with their eyes blown out! Do you think that's better than running a business that employs 2,500 people?'

'You're preaching to the converted.'

My response takes him by surprise. As he surveys me with his piercing pale eyes, Sabatini certainly doesn't cut the figure of a doddering old patriarch. With his sun-kissed Mediterranean skin, barely greyed temples and brooding charm, he's a man in the prime of life. He could easily be the poster boy for AcquaAlta's luxury clothing himself.

'I've grown this business, like my father and grandfather before me, and like the five generations before them. I had every right to expect Marco to play his part.'

'But there are other family members who could take up the reins, aren't there? Bianca told me you have two brothers and a sister who have children too.'

'It's not the same,' he insists. 'They're not *my* children. I'd hoped Marco would come round eventually. That he'd toughen up. That once he got older, he'd be proud of what our family had built.'

'But Marco couldn't have pulled off a turnaround like that. I prettied things up a bit for Bianca, but the truth is that he'd never got over his drug problem. He needed a guardian angel watching over him twenty-four-seven.'

L'Ingegnere rubs his eyes.

'At least you're honest, and I appreciate what you did for

97

Marco. His funeral will be in Tortona, on our family estate. If you'd like to join us, you'd be welcome.'

'Of course I'll come.'

I pause before playing the pivotal card in my plan.

'Your son had his qualities too, Mr Sabatini. Despite your differences, he had a lot of respect for you and it pained him that you'd drifted apart. Yes, he had his problems, but it wasn't all doom and gloom.'

In turn, I take from my bag an image that I've spent days perfecting on Photoshop. A black-and-white shot of me and Marco on a deserted beach.

I hold out the photograph to Sabatini.

'This was taken three weeks ago, in Normandy. We were so happy.'

He stares at it for a long time, motionless, inevitably noticing his son's hand on my stomach.

'I'm expecting Marco's child,' I tell him.

My words floor him. As if I've been hiding a grenade in my bag the whole time, and I've just pulled out the pin.

'I swear to you, I'm not expecting anything from your family. I'd never dream of asking you for money. I'll raise this child alone and—'

'Wait, wait,' he implores, placing his hand on my forearm.

I know he's thinking at lightning speed. That he woke up this morning convinced the days ahead – the *years* ahead – would be gruelling. Joyless. One long, bitter night. But suddenly, a change in the wind might just have opened a chink of light amid the storm clouds. *Buon tempo e mal tempo non dura tutto il tempo.* Good weather and bad weather don't last forever.

I know that, like me, Sabatini is alive to *kairos*. Like me, he's sensing that from nowhere, life is throwing him a chance to turn the tide. A heaven-sent solution to his woes: a final reconciliation with his son, and an heir to succeed him one day at the helm of AcquaAlta. As long as he's able to snatch it. Now or never.

'That's wonderful news, *Angelica*!'

I give the flicker of a smile.

'We'll do this right. I can pull a few strings in Turin, make sure Marco's officially recognised as the father. If you're happy with that, of course.'

At my nod, *L'Ingegnere* rises from his seat and takes me in his arms.

'You're one of the family now.'

3

The same day
11.30 p.m.

I'd naively assumed that only your first murder really bites. The one that initiates you into the realm of killers. The next time around – should the need arise – I thought it would just be one more stroke on the tally sheet.

Clearly, that's not how it works. But I don't have a choice. Now that I've pushed the first domino, the chain has fallen into motion. To keep control of my fate, I need to kill again. In my sights tonight: Stella Petrenko. The woman who started everything, and in whose hands it could all come tumbling down.

In under ten days, I've achieved the impossible. I saw an

opening and I dived in head first. I pushed my luck with a wild, brazen gamble. I went all in, and now I'm about to scoop the pot. Petrenko is the final obstacle in my path.

I know how things will go if I do nothing. The old ballerina will get increasingly nasty as she sees my plan coming to fruition. She'll never stop demanding more and more money. Whatever I do, wherever I go, she'll be the sword of Damocles hanging over my head.

Yet, as I crouch on the zinc roof, I tell myself that this is the last hurdle to clear. With Stella dead, I'll be free.

So that she wouldn't know I was back, I took the service stairs up to Marco's flat. Then I climbed out of one of the dormers, nearly breaking my neck in the process, and crept along the guttering. And for the past forty-five minutes, I've been waiting.

To begin with I was shaking like mad, terrified of falling to my death. Now my legs are tingling with pins and needles. At one point a random flight of seagulls almost sent me hurtling down all six floors, but I managed to steady myself in the nick of time. Contrary to what I'd feared, I'm not particularly on show up here. It's a far cry from *Rear Window.* In the block opposite, the only lights I can see are on the second floor. That's something that has always struck me – how many empty flats there are in Paris. Tough shit for all the rough sleepers; all the better for me. With only half an hour until midnight, it's starting to get late, and the 7th arrondissement isn't the liveliest part of the city. Without seeing him, I can hear the owner of the bar on the corner whistling as he clears the chairs from the terrace.

From my slate-and-zinc vantage point, I have a direct view over Stella Petrenko's terrace. She's slumped in her wing chair, dolled up like mutton dressed as lamb in her tights, tutu and leotard. Earlier on she rolled herself a joint, cackling away as she washed it down with three straight glasses of Burgundy, before conking out for twenty minutes.

At last, she staggers to her feet. She rubs her neck and leans over the balcony, murmuring an old aria:

> There once was a king of Thule
> Who, faithful unto the grave,
> Kept in memory of his love
> A vessel of chiselled gold . . .

My heart's thrashing in my chest. A lump barrels up my throat.

Now.

I jump. A drop of over six feet, but it's doable. I land on the terrace with both hands plastered to the floor. I spring to my feet again.

Stella tries to turn around, but I grab her by the knees and lift her with all my might over the balcony rail. Her howl of protest remains frozen on her lips.

Too late.

She's already splattered across the pavement.

I toss the watering can onto the street and scale the guard-rail to get back onto the roof.

It wasn't so hard, in the end.

III

MATHIAS TAILLEFER

10

WITHOUT A TRACE

1

Wednesday, 29 December

Mathias Taillefer tugged up his coat collar as he left the train station. Despite his hangover, the cop had forced himself to get up early, shave and throw on a clean shirt and jacket. He'd picked up the RER B line from the Cité Universitaire stop, not far from his house. Then a half-hour's trek across Paris and out to Aulnay-sous-Bois.

While he paused on the forecourt to spark up, he punched into his iPhone the address that Nora Messaoud had given him for Angélique Charvet. He took a few fervent drags, as if the tobacco had the power to fuel him to life, then consulted the route suggested by the GPS.

Ten a.m. Although the sky was crystal clear, everywhere was deadened by the arctic cold. Over the festive break, the area had lost a good chunk of its residents. Under the sunlit winter glaze, the centre of Aulnay-sous-Bois had a confused cinematic quality – like a cross between the bygone 14th arrondissement of Michel Audiard and the gritty nineties suburbs of Mathieu Kassovitz's *La Haine*.

Gradually, the cop regained his bearings. He'd first visited the place ten or fifteen years earlier, as part of an investigation. Nothing much had changed. Asian grocers were rolling up their shutters along Route de Bondy, sleepy-eyed supermarket bouncers were smoking in front of the Monoprix, a group of bored youths were loitering by the community centre. On Boulevard de Strasbourg it was market day, and the remaining locals were rushing to stock up on New Year's Eve provisions. The atmosphere around the stalls was tense. Masks, gel and social distancing were back in force as a new variant rocked the country. The previous evening, the number of infections had topped 200,000 for the first time. Two days away from the countdown to 2022, Omicron was tearing French families apart again – mandatory self-isolation, clashes between pro- and anti-vaxxers, increasingly tough restrictions on movement.

Struggling to catch his breath, Taillefer ducked into a pharmacy for some esomeprazole and Aspirin-C tablets. He'd woken that morning with crippling heartburn. His neck was killing him, his head felt like a dead weight and his morale was through the floor. More uncharacteristically, he couldn't focus. His thoughts kept swelling, scattering, stealing away. Then there was the dizziness – reality felt fuzzier, the world seeming to float around him. And to cap it all, the racing beat of his heart, pounding with the question: *What if I've caught this bastard virus too?*

As a transplant patient, he'd been one of the first to receive the vaccine. For people like him, the mortality risk was multiplied by being on immunosuppressants. So far he'd pushed the worst of his worries aside, persuaded that fear of the virus was worse than the virus itself, but the latest twist in the crisis changed the rules of the game.

On his way out of the pharmacy, he stopped at a kiosk on the market to buy a couple of croissants and a small bottle of water. He was craving a coffee too, but his stomach had other ideas. He could practically hear it muttering, 'Don't even try it.' As he swallowed his pills, his phone vibrated. *Louise Collange*. He made no attempt to pick up. The last thing he needed was that kid in his hair.

He pressed on until he reached a small burrstone building on the corner of Place du Général-Leclerc and Rue Jacques Chirac. Two uninspiring floors topped by a crow-stepped gable roof, with a frontage blackened by pollution.

Mathias didn't waver long. Creaking open the gate, he climbed the front steps to a dated wooden door with a fussy wrought-iron grille. There were two buzzers: the first in the name of Angélique Charvet, and the second belonging to someone called Beatriz Barros. The place was quiet, but his cop's instinct warned of potential danger. To soothe his doubts, he patted his SIG Sauer in its Velcro holster.

Before his finger had even hit the buzzer, the door swung back to reveal an otherworldly creature. A six-and-a-half-foot giant of a man, with wavy blond hair and bloated features bulging out from behind a twin-filter respirator mask.

'What do you want?' the giant demanded.

The nasal, cartoonish squeal jarred with his physique, as if the guy had just shot up on laughing gas.

'Mathias Taillefer, Major Crime Unit. And you are?'

'József Vigazs, the owner.'

A small woman appeared behind him. Four-and-a-half-foot tall, dark hair, and a face like a feral mouse.

'Ask for his badge, József.'

Taillefer felt a stab of irritation.

'Who are you, madam?'

'Mónika Vigazs, his mother.'

The cop rubbed his eyes. He could sense the pair weren't going to make things easy for him.

'I'm looking for Angélique Charvet.'

'She doesn't live here anymore.'

'Let's talk inside,' he insisted. 'It's cold out here.'

But He-Man and his old dear stood firm in the doorway, determined not to give an inch.

Taillefer unbuttoned his jacket to show them the holster containing his semi-automatic and the handcuffs looped to his belt.

'Or we can go to the Paris Judicial Police HQ. Rue de Bastion, Batignolles quarter. It's a new building, I can give you the tour.'

The threat held, and the two guard dogs grudgingly sloped aside.

2

Taillefer strode into the first-floor flat. Judging by the tarpaulin-sheathed parquet, stepladders, trestles and paint pots, the place was undergoing a full-scale makeover. Its layout was one step up from a bedsit, with a sofa, a bed and a smattering of other furniture protected by polythene sheets.

'Is this where Angélique Charvet lived?'

'Yes,' József confirmed, after exchanging glances with his mother.

He'd removed his dust mask to reveal his unfortunate looks in all their glory – flat-top haircut, bovine stare and fleshy rosacea-flushed cheeks.

'She cancelled the lease in mid-September,' the mouse explained. 'Then the woman upstairs did the same a month later. We're taking the opportunity to renovate the place. We're missing the extra income, but that's life.'

'Did Angélique Charvet give an address when she left?'

'No, nothing. The skank didn't even bother doing the inventory. She can wave goodbye to her deposit, that's for sure!'

Appearance-wise, the woman was at the opposite end of the spectrum to her son. Barely seven stone wringing wet, straight hair framing a gaunt face, hawkish dark eyes and a clarion voice. It was hard to believe they were related.

'Why are the police interested in her?'

Taillefer dodged the question.

'What kind of tenant was she?' he asked.

The mouse gave a hollow laugh.

'The bad-payer kind. She needed constant chasing for the rent.'

'Did she live alone?'

'I think so,' József replied. 'At least, whenever I came over to fix anything, it was always just her.'

Taillefer wandered through the living space.

'Is the furniture hers?'

'No, the flat was rented fully furnished. Only the books are hers.'

He stopped by the bookcase and lifted the plastic sheet to examine the contents. Classic and contemporary fiction, essay collections, books on art, sociology and medicine,

109

fashion magazines. Angélique was a voracious reader with eclectic tastes. He also clocked several framed photographs on the shelves. Artful selfies playing with the proportions of her face, mapping the fifty shades of Angélique from sleek blonde fringe to shaggy auburn bob. A dazzling portrait of twenty-first-century egotism, of a loner who preferred to stage herself rather than rely on the gaze of others. A girl capable of slipping on multiple identities. An ever-changing chameleon. *A danger, perhaps . . .*

As he approached the back window, he noticed a broken pane that had been patched up with a binbag. Leaning closer, he saw that two slats of the shutter had been wrenched off.

'Was there a break-in?'

'If there's one thing not lacking around here, it's scum,' Mónika Vigazs said sourly.

'When did it happen?'

'After Charvet left, I imagine. Unless she smashed it herself and decided to keep schtum.'

'Did Angélique leave anything else? Clothes? Paperwork?'

'The main thing that sow left was a godawful mess,' the landlady replied with a wet sniff.

Wiping the trail of mucus on her sleeve, she pointed to a pair of industrial bins across the street.

'The place hadn't been cleaned and there was rubbish spilling everywhere.'

The cop frowned.

'So . . . you only began clearing the flat today?'

'We started two days ago, but we still haven't finished. Because of the bank holidays the recycling hasn't been collected yet, so it's all down there.'

Too good to be true. Taillefer scampered out of the

110

building and over the road. Thrusting open the two containers, he tipped the contents onto the pavement and began rifling through. It was a thankless task, and even he didn't really know what he was looking for, but he was determined to leave no stone unturned.

Angélique Charvet's rubbish was in no way remarkable. The woman didn't seem hung up on her eco credentials and liked her online shopping. The haul was strewn with boxes and packaging from trendy fashion brands like Sézane and Rouje, as well as sizeable quantities of Corona cans, plastic water bottles, batteries and polystyrene packing chips. After ten minutes of exploration, Taillefer took a breather. The icy air was freezing his lungs and making his whole body tremble. His forehead, on the other hand, was molten, as if his brain were undergoing nuclear fusion. Even if he'd evidently overestimated what the exercise might yield, he rubbed his hands together and steeled himself to keep going. He ran his gaze over the mound of paperwork he'd set aside – payslips, bills, rent receipts, Crédit Mutuel bank statements. The documents spoke of a financial situation that was tottering, but not earth-shattering.

Suddenly, his eyes were drawn by a torn-up, handwritten letter – the sort people used to send each other before technology cannibalised our lives. Tossing away his cigarette butt, he knelt on the pavement to slot back together the pieces. It was a rambling missive, addressed to Angélique by a besotted lover – someone calling himself Corentin Lelièvre. Taillefer strained to decipher the cursive script. The bloke had obviously got it bad. His treacly prose maundered on about his agony at being rejected by his beloved, imploring the nurse to give him another chance. The cop pocketed the letter.

It stirred in him a mixture of disgust and pity. Perhaps he was mistaken, but he couldn't picture Charvet with a soppy scribbler who seemed lost in a bygone age. Getting to his feet, he brushed off his jacket and trousers and began putting the remaining rubbish back in the bins.

He knew he wouldn't find anything more. In the train that morning, he'd established that Angélique Charvet had a minimal online presence. Nora Messaoud had sworn she'd seen an Instagram profile at one point, but it must have been deleted.

The bird had flown. For good.

As he reached for the last cardboard box, he tried to show off by shooting it into the container, slam-dunk style, but the box bounced off the side and onto the pavement. It was while scooping up the contents that he noticed a plastic stick. At first he thought it was an old Covid test, but as he examined it more closely, he realised his error. It was a pregnancy test. Positive.

Taillefer closed the bin lid pensively, then disinfected himself with a long squirt of hand sanitiser – now wasn't the time to fall ill. He couldn't resist smiling. Five years after being cast out of the force, he finally had a new case to solve. The trail was faint, but intriguing. He was no stranger to stepping into the unknown, into a whorl of out-of-focus images and tangled threads that initially seemed impossible to unravel. None of that daunted him. Sooner or later, something would come along to restore order to the chaos. But where could he find that missing piece of the puzzle? In Stella Petrenko's flat? He'd been too cursory during his first visit. Out of decency, he hadn't dug as deeply as he should have. But there was always round two.

3

Louise flicked on her indicator light and nosed into Rue de Bellechasse. For the first time since she'd been coming there, she had the pick of parking spots. Never had she seen Paris so empty, purged of tourists and anaesthetised by the pandemic. With their sparse Christmas decorations, the streets of the Saint-Thomas-d'Aquin quarter reminded her of a film set. Cinecittà minus the cast.

After parking right on the corner of Rue Las-Cases, she slipped into the deserted building and called the lift up to the fifth floor. She'd barely slept a wink, too agitated by the lack of progress in her 'investigation'. Weary of groping in the dark, she'd resolved to confront her mother's ghost head-on. And to do that, she needed to brave the murky waters of Stella Petrenko's private life. In practical terms, this meant turning the flat inside out, without fear of unearthing the 'wretched little pile of secrets' that each of us carries inside.

Louise locked the door behind her and dumped her rucksack on a chair. Despite the sunlight spilling across the parquet, the flat was icy. After switching on the radiators at full blast, she rehung the Sabatini portrait on the wall, then filled the coffee machine and brewed herself a long espresso while she waited for the place to heat up. A little earlier, she'd tried phoning Taillefer to ask for his help, but the cop had blanked her call. Oh well, she was bright enough to manage without him.

She sipped her coffee and stared into space, mulling over the struggles and disappointments that had defined her mother's story. From being tiny, Stella Petrenko's existence had been devoted to a single goal: becoming a Paris Opera prima ballerina. With hindsight, Louise recognised this as the root of all the frustrations that had blighted her mother's life. The stark truth was that all her sacrifices, all those hours of graft, had spawned more pain than joy. Very quickly, Stella had learnt that she wasn't the most beautiful, graceful or gifted dancer. But she'd climbed each rung by hook or by crook, clawing her way to the crown of prima ballerina. For as long as she could remember, Louise had always heard her mother saying she'd made it 'by the skin of her teeth'.

The tragedy for Stella was that she didn't just want to be liked, she wanted to be *the favourite*. Because she genuinely believed she was more deserving than anyone else. Her Ukrainian roots, her family's upheaval to Marseille, her ten-hour days of training, her battered body, her accident, her injuries. Stella had never danced without hurting somewhere. Her career had been one long martyrdom, but for what? She'd barely fluttered her frail wings in the firmament before she was forced to relinquish her crown and fade into oblivion.

Her retirement from the Opera had propelled her on a downward spiral, and the teaching post she'd subsequently taken up at the Ménagerie de Verre theatre hadn't come close to reversing her fall. Contemporaries like Marie-Agnès Gillot, Aurélie Dupont, Sylvie Guillem and Marie-Claude Pietragalla had all succeeded in reinventing themselves to stay at the top. Not Stella Petrenko. As someone who'd always teetered on the brink of collapse, both physical and emotional, Stella was floored by the chasm she now faced. How could life have dared to snatch from her so quickly what she'd spent years teasing from its grasp?

Louise had worried for Stella. Her mother hadn't built any reserves. Since Laurent Collange, no man had really hung around in her life. Every time she visited, Louise found her mother lonely and unhappy, seething with resentment and polluted by a bitterness that she was increasingly unable to contain.

The strangest part was that Stella wasn't even Louise's real mother. Her 'genetrix' – as Louise's father preferred to call her – was in fact a former flautist from the Radio France Orchestra. An unstable woman with a chequered history, who'd been in and out of psychiatric hospitals in Germany and the Netherlands. She'd been together with Louise's father in the early 2000s, and had fallen pregnant by accident.

After much wavering, she'd grudgingly decided to keep the baby. The pregnancy had been an ordeal, and the infant's arrival had only made matters worse. A fortnight after the birth, she'd left for Berlin, abandoning her newborn daughter with her partner. For a time she'd shared a squat with a group of militants from Apokalypse, a German civil disobedience movement which railed against state inaction on animal rights and climate change.

After that Laurent Collange had lost touch with her, never to see her again. Stella had come into his life when Louise was six months old, and the ballerina had raised Louise as if she were her own. There'd been no deceit as such, but as the flautist had never returned to see her daughter, she'd simply vanished from the family's thoughts and conversations. Until the day in 2010 when Laurent Collange received a call from the Netherlands, informing him that his ex-partner had died of breast cancer in a Rotterdam hospital. A sad end to a sorry life. Louise's father had waited until his daughter was fifteen to reveal the truth about her birth mother's fate. But the story that had lingered in the margins of Louise's childhood and adolescence hadn't changed her feelings towards Stella Petrenko. As far as Louise was concerned, she had no other mother. She'd nonetheless made the trip to Rotterdam the previous year to meet her biological grandmother, but the visit had fallen flat. They had nothing to say to each other. No shared past. Ultimately, the cool indifference of the Dutch had only reinforced Louise's valuing of her upbringing and love for Stella, who, for all her faults, would always be her one and only mother.

4

After rinsing her cup in the sink, the young woman buckled down to the task she'd set herself: searching the place from top to bottom. Like in the raids she'd seen in police dramas, she dismantled the toilet cistern, checked the floorboards, flung open drawers, rummaged through piles of clothes, examined the contents of cupboards, pored over the paperwork on the desk, inspected the oven and extractor fan, unscrewed lightbulbs, prodded the ceiling, knocked on walls, until . . .

A hollow sound in the dividing wall of the semi-open kitchen piqued her attention. After managing to pivot one of the frosted-glass panes, she discovered a small cubbyhole between the two panels. As she angled her phone torch over it, she saw that someone had hidden two envelopes inside.

There are no secrets time will not reveal, she thought to herself, feeding her hand into the gap to catch the envelopes between her middle and index fingers. The first, made of sturdy, white laid paper, was stuffed with wads of fifty-euro notes. Emptying it onto the granite worktop, Louise quickly totted up the spoils. Ten thousand euros exactly. *Savings?* On closer inspection of the envelope, she noticed an embossed stamp in one corner – a monogram featuring two inter-locking Bs. She'd seen the motif before: it was the logo of Bernard Benedick Gallery. *Payment for a Sabatini portrait Stella had sold him, perhaps?* But if that were the case, why hadn't the gallery owner mentioned it to her?

The second envelope, smaller than the first, contained only a memory stick. Louise retrieved her laptop from her rucksack and sat down at the desk in the living room. With a knot of apprehension, she slid the device into the USB port. There was a single, unnamed folder. Inside it were a dozen video files, each under three minutes long. Clicking one of them at random, she clapped her hands to her mouth as the opening frames rolled into view. The footage, filmed from a distance, showed her mother in the throes of passion with a man she didn't recognise. Louise opened the second clip, then the third . . .

All the videos were similar in tone. Only her mother's sexual partner changed each time. With a monumental effort, Louise tried to view the footage objectively. First up, there was no hint of assault. Nor did Stella seem to be under the influence. But this wasn't simply a collection of sex tapes that the dancer had amassed over the years. For one thing, the videos were recent, all of them dating from the past few months. For another, the setting was always the same – the living-room sofa. Lastly, they'd all been recorded from afar, using some kind of long-focus lens expressly trained on . . .

the room where she was sitting at that very moment. Louise slammed down the screen and scanned around her. The sun had vanished behind a bank of dark clouds, plunging the flat into deepening shadows. *Shit.* Louise sensed she was being watched. Whoever had filmed the scenes with her mother could only have done so from a vantage point *on the other side of the street.* She raced to pull the curtains across the French windows, then took refuge in the kitchen, fear swelling inside her. She'd smugly thought herself clever with her plan to search the flat, but someone else was pulling the strings. A puppet-master who, right then, was no doubt having a good laugh behind his window.

She stayed there for a long time, frozen in the silent flat. Who could have filmed the videos? And more pressingly, why? To blackmail her mother? But in what way was the footage compromising? Stella had always had a colourful love life, and she'd made no bones about it. The sinister silence persisted, then was abruptly broken by the purr of the lift being called from the lower floors. What if whoever had been watching her was back to claim his dues? No, the thought was totally irrational. Even so, Louise cowered in the corner of the kitchen, listening intently. The lift's growl became louder, then stopped on the fifth floor. *Shiiit.*

Louise heard heavy footsteps advancing along the corridor. Then she saw the front door handle being rammed down, and the wood shuddering against the intruder's force. She bit down on her fist to stop herself screaming. *What could she do?*

A fresh silence descended, followed by a metallic clicking sound. The guy was trying to pick the lock. This time, the danger was too real. '*Help! Help!*' Louise shrieked, again and again. Her cries only drove the attacker to move faster, and to switch tactics. Now, he was intent on breaking the door down. His first two blows nearly smashed the panels, then a third wrenched the door from its hinges and burst the lock. Louise dived under the kitchen counter. With a final kick the wood surrendered, and a male silhouette appeared in the doorway.

It was Mathias Taillefer.

11

HIKIKOMORI

1

'You scared me to death, for fuck's sake!' Louise fumed as she re-emerged from her hiding place.

'It was *you* who scared me,' Taillefer protested. 'Why did you start screaming like that?'

Making his way into the flat, he examined the wreckage of the door and tried vainly to wedge it back in place.

'What the fuck are you doing here?' the young woman shrilled.

'Calm down.'

'Why didn't you answer my calls?'

'I've brought croissants,' he ventured, waving the paper bag he'd been ferrying around since leaving the market in Aulnay.

'You can shove your croissants up your arse!'

She flounced off to the bathroom and slammed the door.

Taillefer sighed. To think that some people were stuck living with teenagers on a daily basis. You really would have to be a glutton for punishment. He stood for a moment warming his hands against the radiator. The pills were starting to kick in. He already felt miles better, readier to face the world. *Three cheers for chemistry*. To seal his return to the land of the living, he even decided to chance a coffee. As he was slotting the capsule in the machine, his gaze fell on the ten thousand euros on the countertop. Where had that kind of cash come from? Then he noticed the gap in the wall, and the unsealed envelope embossed with the letters 'BB'. *Bernard Benedick*, he realised, making the mental link. Louise Collange had stolen a march on him in searching the flat.

'Come back!' he called. 'I've got news for you.'

No response. While he waited, he hooked up his phone to the Wi-Fi printer and ran off a photo of Angélique Charvet. A black-and-white screenshot of her LinkedIn profile pic-ture – the only trace of the nurse he'd found online.

Louise left him hanging for a good three minutes before deigning to appear, still looking tetchy. By way of peace-offering, Taillefer gave her the lowdown on the Angélique Charvet lead that he'd traced back to Aulnay-sous-Bois.

'Maybe you met her when you were visiting your mum?'

Louise shook her head. Taillefer twigged that she was in shock.

'Did you find anything else in the wall?'

'A USB stick.'

She went to retrieve her laptop from the desk, then set the first video playing.

Taillefer goggled, understanding why the girl had been in such a state when he arrived.

'The other videos are basically the same,' Louise told him. 'Only the partner changes each time.'

The cop instinctively pulled out his phone and took three

shots of the footage. He scratched his head. The case was taking a new, unanticipated turn. The whole thing smacked of blackmail, of other people's dirty laundry . . . The kind of stuff he'd never felt comfortable with. But what bothered him most was the camera angle.

He leapt up and rushed out onto the terrace. By a trick of the light, his eyes were drawn to a window in the building opposite where the shutter had just been lowered. In the exact same spot that he'd seen the reflection the previous afternoon.

'You stay here,' he said, turning to Louise. 'I'm off to pay a visit to our Peeping Tom.'

'No way, I'm coming with you.'

'No – it could be dangerous. There's no knowing what kind of nutter we might find and—'

'You'll protect me,' she cut in, nodding at the holster containing his SIG Sauer.

Taillefer pulled a face, but he didn't waste his breath trying to reason with her. *Finally, a slice of action!* He felt rejuvenated, raring for battle. Bolting down the stairs, he charged across the street like a mad dog and started buzzing the intercoms of all the flats in the block opposite, snarling out his favourite line: 'Police! Open up! Police!'

2

At last the door clicked open. With Louise trailing in his wake, Taillefer bypassed the lift and streaked up to the fifth floor. A woman was waiting for them with a wary expression, half-hidden in the crack of the doorway.

The cop had noted the name on the buzzer downstairs: Carine Leblan. A haggard-looking fifty-something with a gingery complexion and bobbed hair, squeezed inside an overtight puffer jacket. Judging by the scarf around her neck, they'd caught her on the hop.

'Mrs Leblan?'

She seemed terror-stricken.

'You're here for Romuald, are you?' she asked in a quavering voice. 'What's he done now?'

Taillefer made to barge his way past.

'Can we come in for a second?'

Without awaiting her reply, he strode into the hallway. It led onto a small, cheerless sitting room, which had clearly seen better days.

'Do you live here?'

'Yes. What do you want with me, for heaven's sake?'

Carine Leblan had already ditched her scarf and unzipped her coat.

'Was it you who took these photos?' Taillefer demanded, foisting his phone screen at her.

'Eurgh! No, it certainly wasn't me!'

'But it's the view from your windows. Do you know who did take them?'

'I suppose it was my son, Romuald,' she sighed.

'Your son? How old is he?'

'Nearly twenty.'

'Is he here?'

'He's in his room, but—'

'I want to speak to him. Now.'

She gave another long sigh.

'Before you see Romuald, I need to give you some context.'

Carine Leblan looked exhausted, as if every word was a struggle. She traipsed off to the kitchen to boil the kettle, while Louise and Taillefer followed behind. The cop was about to launch into another question, but a pointed look from Louise told him to keep schtum.

'Would you both like a tea?'

'Please,' the young woman replied.

Taillefer mumbled an inaudible response that Carine decided to take for a 'yes'. She laid three cups on the table.

'My husband taught French at a secondary school on the outskirts of Paris,' she began, her eyes fixed on the bubbling water. 'Like a lot of teachers, he found it hard to cope with all the changes in the profession and the way the state education system had been left to rot. These past ten years he was like an empty shell – utterly burnt-out with it all.'

Carine Leblan spoke in a small voice, clearly choked.

'He felt he'd been treated like scum. He was constantly asking: "How have we come to this?" He used to be very active in the Socialist Party, back in the day, but he was so disillusioned with how the left had been taken over by identity politics, he ended up severing ties with his old political crowd. He despaired at how splintered society had become, how everything was going to pot. It cut him to the bone. He didn't understand how people had lost the ability to talk to each other, why they couldn't rub along and work to find solutions together.'

The light on the kettle clicked off. Taillefer was growing impatient. Carine took three muslin teabags from a box and placed them in the cups.

'In January 2020, on a Monday morning, my husband killed himself on the school grounds after a run-in with a student. The case got a lot of attention. Some sick little bastards filmed the scene and shared it on social media. My son was destroyed by what happened. He's barely left his room since his father's death.'

Louise's eyes widened. Taillefer remained unmoved.

'My son's never been particularly sociable. He's spent the past decade glued to his screens. He's bright, but his obsession with computers has led him to do all kinds of stupid things. Perhaps you know this, but he's already got a criminal record.'

Taillefer masked his surprise with a slow, knowing nod. Carine continued.

'In his last year of sixth form, he hacked into Parcoursup, the government portal that manages higher-education places, so that he could impress a girl he liked by getting her onto the course she wanted.'

She poured the boiling water over the teabags before resuming in a fatalistic tone.

'But now, things have reached a new level. Romuald's given up on his studies. He doesn't have any friends, and he's completely out of social circulation. For two years he's been holed up in his room, doing nothing but sleeping, watching series and scrolling the internet. Some days he doesn't even open the curtains. He can go for a week without washing, just urinating in plastic bottles. He refuses to see a psychologist, but I'm at my wits' end. I'm scared that the damage is too deep, and that he'll never get back to a normal life.'

While Louise was transfixed by the tale, Taillefer was less convinced. He'd spent years reading about *hikikomori* – the young recluses who lived as modern-day hermits in Japan.

Each time, the same thought crossed his mind: *they want a damn good kick up the arse.*

'Why don't you give him a good shaking?' he asked, blowing on his tea.

'Because violence is always the answer . . .' Carine Leblan murmured.

'Chuck him out and cut off his allowance,' Taillefer huffed. 'You'll see how quickly he finds his social skills again. Anyway, this doesn't get him out of being questioned.'

'Question him by all means, but go gently. Oh, and one last thing: Romuald can't stand the police.'

3

Spoiling for a fight, Taillefer pushed open the door to the geek's lair. His first surprise was the generous proportions of the room. The kid had clearly claimed the plummest room in the flat – a 200-square-foot starship with a knockout view over the rooftops.

His second surprise was the size of Leblan. He'd expected him to be built like a basketball player, but Romuald was a stunted specimen who didn't look his twenty years. With his unbuttoned denim shirt splayed over a Foo Fighters T-shirt, he came across as a flabby, ill-bred schoolboy. A spotty, bespectacled teenager with a dodgy bowl cut poking out from under a baseball cap and shifty, globular eyes. Luckily, he seemed to have washed recently and there were no bottles of piss in the vicinity.

'Hi Romuald, I'm Louise,' the young woman began.

Leblan rubbed his eyes. He was sitting barefoot in sliders,

facing three huge screens that were arranged in a semi-circle around a sticker-covered MacBook Pro. He must have over-heard his mother talking with the cop, but seemed surprised to discover the girl.

'And I'm the police,' Taillefer announced.

While the two adolescents stared at each other, slightly entranced, Mathias took the chance to explore the room. The walls were plastered with film posters, some of classics that he recognised – *Close Encounters of the Third Kind*, *Robocop* – and others he'd never heard of, like *The Prestige* and *Welcome to Zombieland*. The shelves were heaving under piles of books, spanning everything from graphic novels, manga and sci-fi to tomes on magic and mentalism. The cop was phobic about clutter, and even with its sprawling dimensions, the room made him feel oppressed. There was too much tat, too many things crammed into the space, from the Gibson Firebird guitar and Roland Juno synth to the chipped Grendizer figurine. Where had the geek got the money for it all?

'It stinks in here!' he shouted, flinging open the window.

An icy blast of wind swept the room.

'Hey, it's freezing!' Romuald protested.

'It'll do you good,' Taillefer replied. 'The fresh air will do wonders for your memory, you'll see.'

Drawing level with the kid, he swiped the cap from his head.

'It's bad manners to wear a hat indoors, young man. Didn't they teach you that in school?'

'That's out of order!' the boy howled, as though he'd just been punched.

Louise eyed Mathias reproachfully, but the cop kept up his goading.

'Does it ever occur to you to clean this place?' he asked, gesticulating at the mound of sweet wrappers, KFC boxes, kebab trays and pop cans spilling from the bin.

Unabashed, he opened the desk drawers to peer inside.

'Oi, that's private! You've no right to snoop through my things!'

'Shut it, fuckface.'

'Why are you even here?' the geek yelled. 'Get off my case, you dirty pig!'

'And what's that, eh?' Taillefer continued, motioning to the telescope that was mounted on a tripod by the window. 'For gazing at the stars, is it? Or ogling your neighbours?'

'I . . .'

'And these videos,' the cop barked, waving his phone in the boy's face. 'Was it you that filmed them, you little shit?'

Romuald Leblan squirmed free of Taillefer's grip, then, after a lengthy reflection, performed a radical turnaround to admit his guilt without the slightest remorse.

'Yeah, it was me, and so what? This is my house. I can do what I want.'

'Did you know her – Stella Petrenko?'

'Obviously. Ever since we moved here.'

'Why did you have these videos of her on a USB stick? Were you blackmailing her?'

'Ha!' the geek snorted. 'The other way round, more like.'

'Go on.'

'It was *her* that asked me to film them.'

'That's a lie!' Louise cried.

Taillefer wasn't sure he'd understood.

'What are you talking about?'

'It was a nice little money-spinner she'd cooked up. She'd

pick up married men – usually blokes from backwaters out-side Paris or old fans, then invite them back to hers and convince them to shag her in the living room.'

'Then you did your Kubrick act from across the street?'

'Kubrick never shot pornos, but yeah, that was the idea.'

'And then you'd ask them for hush money to stop the videos getting out . . .'

'Nothing gets past you, gramps.'

The geek had his swagger back.

'Pretty sordid,' Taillefer frowned.

Romuald shrugged. 'It was just a bit of fun.'

'You make me sick!' Louise burst in, visibly shaken.

'All right! No one died!'

'That's the whole point, actually. Stella did.'

Romuald resumed his cross-legged slouch in his armchair.

'How's that connected? She fell off her balcony and smashed her head in.'

'Someone could have pushed her, though, couldn't they?' Taillefer pressed, gesturing to the Paris skyline beyond the window. 'On the evening she died, did you notice anything unusual?'

'No, they already asked me that.'

'Who did?'

'You should know, shouldn't you? One of your lot – a woman. Senegalese, I think. She came to question everyone in the block the day after the accident.'

Fatoumata Diop, the cop from the Left Bank Judicial Police.

Taillefer edged closer to the window and sparked up. The kid intrigued him, bringing to mind a fat cat lolling in lordly luxury. Thanks to the internet and his computers, the boy wasn't cut off from the world at all. He'd just retreated into

129

his cosseted little bubble. As if staring at a perverse photo negative, Romuald's cushy set-up cast him back to his own teenage self. Montpellier, the high-rises of La Paillade. How many weekends and school holidays had he spent with his dad on building sites as a mere fourteen-year-old? Afternoons spent breaking his back under the blazing sun to bring home a few extra francs. The memories stung, and they'd left him with a lifelong loathing for layabouts like Leblan.

Louise picked up the questioning.

'All those men you blackmailed, maybe one of them wanted to get their own back?'

'Nah, they were just losers from the back of beyond. We only ever asked them for piddling amounts – fifteen hundred, two thousand euros – and they always paid up.'

'Send me all the names anyway,' Taillefer ordered, scrawling his email address on a Post-it note. 'What were you doing on the night of Stella's death?'

Romuald sighed theatrically, fiddling with his AirPods case.

'I've already said it all, man.'

'Well say it again, dickhead.'

'I was watching the match on TV – Belgium versus Czech Republic.'

'Not the sexiest match in the world, is it?'

'My mum's Belgian. I've got dual nationality. And they're a fucking good team, the Red Devils.'

'They get a lot of the ball, but no end product. That's about right, isn't it?'

Romuald's patience frayed. 'Look, have you come to talk football or . . . ?'

'What time does a match finish?' Taillefer continued. 'Half-ten, eleven? What did you do afterwards?'

'I played online with my headphones on until the pigs and the paramedics rocked up outside and started screeching the place down.'

Taillefer stamped out his cigarette butt and tossed it out of the window. Sly, manipulative, but no fool: he could sense the kid was an important piece of the jigsaw. A lemon that he hadn't yet squeezed hard enough. Then he had a stroke of inspiration.

'Do you recognise this woman?' he asked, holding out his phone which was on its last dregs of charge.

'She's not bad,' Romuald smirked after glancing at the screen. 'What's her name?'

'Angélique Charvet. Have you seen her before?'

'She was there the day the ambulance came for the painter that died of Covid – Marco Pantani.'

'Marco Sabatini,' Louise corrected.

'Yeah, him. She spent ages talking to a paramedic who had a face like the back end of a bus.'

Subtle to a fault.

'Was it her who called them?'

'Maybe, I dunno.'

'And have you seen her since then?'

'Oh yeah, that's the weirdest part . . . she came back the same evening.'

'Back where?'

'To the painter's flat. She sat on the terrace and started knocking back drinks, as chilled as you like, as if she owned the place.'

Taillefer was dubious.

'Are you sure of what you're saying?'

'Positive. I saw her necking vodka from the bottle.'

'Why didn't you mention it to the police?'

'None of my business.'

'Maybe she was Marco's girlfriend?' Louise suggested.

'No, he didn't have a girlfriend,' sniggered Romuald. 'Trust me.'

'How can you be so certain?'

'Sabatini was gay. He often brought guys back to his studio – and not just to show them his paintings. But I never saw any girls, and it wasn't for want of looking.'

Louise and Taillefer exchanged a glance: the account didn't square with what Bernard Benedick had said. The gallery owner clearly had something to hide. He was the next person they needed to question again.

'Right, gramps, am I under arrest or what?' the geek sneered.

Taillefer sighed.

'I've no sympathy for little turds like you. Your mother's sick with worry because of the way you're carrying on. You should be ashamed of what you're doing to her. Instead of looking after her, you're driving her to an early grave.'

'Jeez, man! Women don't want looking after anymore – it's nearly 2022, not 1952!'

'Don't get smart with me, bell-end.'

'Or what?'

'Or I'll smash your head in.'

'Yeah, right! You'd be out of a job before the end of the day.'

Taillefer pressed his face up to the geek's.

'I've not been a cop for years, you little twat. Only a

fuckwit like you could have believed I was. I can beat the daylights out of you whenever I want.'

'Ooh, I'm shitting myself.'

Louise stepped in to defuse the situation.

'Come on, Mathias, let's go.'

But Taillefer already had hold of the geek's collar.

'Eat that, zombie!' he bellowed, as he hurled him across the room.

12

PLACE DE L'ÉTOILE

1

Early afternoon

Place de l'Étoile was unrecognisable. For the past three weeks, the Arc de Triomphe had been wrapped in silvery-blue fabric and parcelled up with red rope. The posthumous installation by the artist Christo and his wife Jeanne-Claude had Parisians divided, but it was the talk of the city.

After pulling out of Avenue de Friedland, Louise swung onto the roundabout and the voiturette wheezed its way into the sea of vehicles. Servicing no fewer than twelve major roads, the traffic circle around the Arc de Triomphe was notoriously the most perilous in France.

'Watch yourself,' said Taillefer. 'The wanker behind us is right up your arse.'

Every time she ventured out here, Louise felt like she was mounting the scaffold. She could never find her bearings, lost in the jumble of avenue names – Wagram, Hoche, Foch, Marceau . . . Distant signifiers of Napoleonic power that in her mind, as in the memories of many of the city's residents, had been swept aside by the scenes of the Gilets Jaunes laying siege to the arch. The wound was still raw, but today, with the winter sun rippling hypnotically off the pleats of fabric, the monument was restored to some of its former glory. In its new, luminous cloak, it almost looked alive.

'Careful of that bus, the driver's going like a lunatic,' Taillefer warned. 'Take the next lane. Where did you say Bernard Benedick lived again?'

'On Avenue Kléber, according to his assistant – number 16. But he might already have left for the airport.'

'Let's get a shift on, then.'

'I'm already at max, Mathias!'

Taillefer was writhing in his seat, unable to hide his impatience. Louise strained to focus. After leaving the geek's bedroom in Rue de Bellechasse, she'd suddenly been bludgeoned by fatigue. And the rules here weren't the same as on other roundabouts, where vehicles already in the flow had priority over those joining. She blinked repeatedly. The vastness of the square was dizzying. The endless lanes of traffic, the blaring horns, the absence of signage and road markings . . .

'Watch out!'

From nowhere, a scooter sliced in front of her. Talk about the law of the jungle! In her panic, hoping to escape the junction as swiftly as possible, Louise made the mistake of trying to overtake the garishly coloured florist's van to her right, but the voiturette skidded on the cobbles and was met by furious honking. Enraged, Taillefer wound down his window and brandished a menacing fist at the van driver.

As the cop was calling the florist every name under the sun, Louise mused to herself that it was nice to have someone there who took your side, even when you were in the wrong. That only made her appreciate it all the more.

'There he is!' she cried.

'What?'

Like shipwreck victims on a threadbare raft, they'd weathered the storm of Place de l'Étoile. Number 16 Avenue Kléber stood just across from the sweeping glass canopy of the Peninsula hotel.

'That's him, Bernard Benedick, in the taxi!' Louise repeated.

Mathias narrowed his eyes. A figure had just dived into a 'Club Affaires' Mercedes as the driver loaded a suitcase into the boot. Louise sped to cut in front of the cab so it couldn't pull out.

Seizing the initiative, Taillefer had already slipped on an old orange 'Police' armband that he'd found at home that morning. It did the job every time. In the heat of the moment, appearances counted as much as reality. He didn't even need a badge; it was enough simply to flash his open wallet and adopt an assured tone.

'Police! Turn off the engine!'

'But—'

'Get out of the car, Mr Benedick.'

'But I'll miss my plane!'

'Not if you answer my questions quickly. It all depends on *you*.'

2

Perched at a table on the terrace of a small neighbouring café, the gallery owner glanced anxiously at his Nautilus.

136

Across from him, Taillefer and Louise had spent the past five minutes playing for time. To ramp up the pressure, the cop had refused to conduct the interview by the taxi, and had insisted on sitting down over a drink.

'I'm calling my lawyer.'

'That's the best way of guaranteeing you miss your plane,' cautioned Taillefer. 'And I don't think there are many direct daily flights to San José.'

'It's the only one,' Benedick admitted.

'Nice time to visit Costa Rica, isn't it, late December? The start of the dry season, right?'

'For God's sake! Are you questioning me or what?'

As his first ace, Taillefer pulled from his pocket the envelope containing the ten thousand euros.

'Can you explain to us where this money came from?'

The gallery owner gulped, mortified at being caught red-handed.

'It's . . . It's part of the money I gave to Marco Sabatini's fiancée.'

'What for?'

'For three of Marco's paintings.'

'What do you mean "part of the money"?'

'She came to show me three portraits — a handsome little selection. I offered to buy them for ten thousand euros each.'

'Cash is so much easier, isn't it? No need to worry about giving the taxman a cut.'

'Are you from Major Crime or the bleeding tax office?'

'Watch your tone, Benedick.'

The gallery owner looked away for a moment, staring at the sunlit buildings opposite.

'I've a waiting list as long as my arm for Marco's paintings,' he continued. 'And since his death, their value's tripled. I'd have been mad to pass up the chance to acquire more.'

'Why are people so into them?'

'Collectors are like sheep: they go wild for whatever's the flavour of the moment.'

'But why the big hoo-ha?'

'Sabatini always painted the same scene, but few artists have managed to capture terror like he did.'

'What do you think he was scared of?'

Benedick shrugged.

'Loneliness, death, Francis Lalanne making a comeback . . . How should I know?'

'And what's the deal with the eyes in his paintings – no pupils or irises, empty and bright like silver?'

'Iridium, actually,' Benedick corrected. 'Empty eyes are nothing new in portraiture. It's a device many artists have adopted – from Modigliani through to Sean Lorenz.'

'Is this Sabatini's fiancée?' Taillefer asked. He reached for his phone to bring up Angélique Charvet's photograph, then saw that the battery was dead. He fell back on the printout of her LinkedIn picture.

'Absolutely,' Benedick confirmed. 'A strange girl – slippery. Impossible to pin down.'

'Do you know where she is now?'

The gallery owner's eyes widened.

'How would I? I've only met the woman once in my life.'

'Angélique Charvet never was Sabatini's fiancée,' Taillefer declared.

As Benedick gave another shrug, the cop turned the screw.

'Sabatini was gay. And I think you knew that.'

'So?!' the gallery owner snorted. 'This is 2021, grandad!

People are allowed more than one sexual preference.'

He downed his espresso, then seemed to realise that Taillefer had nothing else on him.

'Anyway, if you've said your piece, I've a plane to catch. By all means send over the desk jockeys from Bercy to check my accounts – but between you and me, something tells me you won't.'

3

Louise cradled her cup between her frozen hands. Her exhaustion had passed, leaving in its wake a state of tension she'd rarely known. In the space of a few hours, her mother's death had been cast in a new light. Like the coloured squares of a Rubik's Cube, seemingly disparate details had begun to align into a coherent whole. And at last, after a session of thrashing out ideas, she and Taillefer were able to reconstruct the plotline of Stella's final days:

Angélique Charvet, an agency nurse who was pregnant with her first child, had been sent to change Stella's dressings at the end of the summer. On 28 August, she'd discovered an ailing Marco Sabatini in the grip of a serious case of Covid. After alerting the paramedics, she'd returned to the painter's flat to steal three paintings, which she'd sold to Benedick while masquerading as Sabatini's fiancée. She'd given part of the money to Stella, then had vanished with the rest. Except that, in the intervening period, Stella had died.

The story had gaps, admittedly, but everything seemed to converge on the mysterious Angélique, the cornerstone of the whole murky puzzle.

'We have a genuine lead!' Louise declared. 'We need to tell your colleagues so they can question Charvet.'

Taillefer was less enthusiastic.

'We can try to find her ourselves.'

'How? She's done a bunk.'

'You don't understand how the police service operates. They won't lift a finger to find her.'

'I can't believe that.'

'They might launch a follow-up investigation in the new year, but it'll take months. We're in France, the most bureaucratic, Kafkaesque country in the world.'

'If you don't want to come with me, I'll go on my own,' she resolved, getting up from her seat.

Taillefer gave a long sigh.

'It's a waste of time, but I'll still come. Otherwise you'll be waiting hours.'

He left a ten-euro note on the table before joining Louise outside.

Along the avenue, sunlight was glistening through the branches of the plane trees. Mathias remained motionless for a moment, his face tilted towards the rays as if they had the power to regenerate him.

'Want me to drive?' he offered, nodding at the voiturette.

'Nah, I'll be fine.'

Taillefer contorted himself into the passenger seat with the same unpleasant sensation of climbing inside a child's toy.

'Your best bet is to head for the 14th arrondissement station,' he concluded, after a moment's reflection, '114 Avenue du Maine.'

'Can you type the address in?' Louise asked, suckering her phone to the windscreen before kicking into gear.

Taillefer obeyed. As the car jolted down Avenue Marceau, an idea came to him.

'I'll try calling Fatoumata Diop, the lieutenant from the Left Bank crew who worked on the investigation,' he announced, taking out his own phone. 'I still have her number.'

While the cop was on the line, Louise retreated into her thoughts. She could feel her eyelids drooping of their own accord, her pupils shrinking under a fresh wave of exhaustion. She'd hadn't eaten anything since the crêpe the previous day, and she was as ravenous as a Tour de France cyclist heaving up Mont Ventoux. She rued spurning Taillefer's croissants, which had been left abandoned in the kitchen. Digging in her coat pocket for anything she could stuff down, she found a lone Biscoff that the waiter had brought with her coffee.

They crossed the Seine over Pont de l'Alma. Absorbed in her ruminations, Louise tried fruitlessly to draw connections between the latest leads they'd gleaned. She was starting to question the point of her search for the truth. Would she truly feel better after solving the mystery of her mother's death?

The green swathes of the Champ de Mars, then the dome of Les Invalides. In the embers of 2021, Paris seemed to be moving in slow motion. The last glimmers of a bleak year that had followed the *annus horribilis* of 2020. The romantics who'd swallowed the fable of 'The World After' were beginning to see that life would simply revert to how it had been before – only worse. The horizon held only gloom and uncertainty. The crazy train had left the station a long time ago. Sometimes people managed to fool themselves there was a way of slamming on the brakes, but that was a fiction.

And deep down, everyone knew it. The fight was lost. The planet would become ever less viable, social media would keep on eroding democracies, the . . .

'We're in luck!' Taillefer trilled as he hung up. 'Not only is Diop on shift for the holidays, but she's at the station all afternoon. She's waiting for us!'

Still wrapped in thought, Louise continued to lurch between visions of the future and musings on the findings of their investigation. Though her head was all over the place, she had the bizarre sense that the picture they'd uncovered so far was only a smokescreen, masking a truth that remained beyond their reach.

'It's always a nightmare finding a parking spot around here,' Taillefer grumbled as they hit the junction of Boulevard du Montparnasse and Avenue du Maine.

An alarm bell sounded in Louise's mind. The imminent eruption of danger.

'Turn here, onto Rue Cels. There's an alley halfway down the street, off to the right. That's where all the local coppers park.'

Flicking on the indicator, Louise carried on for a hundred yards, then veered onto a cobbled lane giving access to a row of small townhouses in the typical pale stone of the 14th arrondissement. It was only as she was manoeuvring to park that she realised what had put her on alert: Taillefer's phone was still out of charge. It had to be. She felt her panic intensify. The ex-cop couldn't have made the call to the station. He'd lied to her.

But why?

They exchanged a look. He saw that she'd understood.

Goosepimples streaked across her legs, chest and forearms,

as it dawned on her that she knew nothing about the man sitting next to her.

'Louise, Louise . . .' he sighed, shaking his head. 'Why didn't you listen to me?'

She should have tried to open the door and run, but she made no attempt to do anything, paralysed by the unreality of what was happening. Taillefer unbuckled his seatbelt.

'Look what a fix you've got us into. I told you to move on. I told you not to stick with me.'

Rooted to her seat, Louise felt a lump blaze up her throat, then a searing pain in her stomach.

'I did tell you I was dangerous.'

The cop's huge hand slammed down to grab her by the neck.

She didn't even struggle. She just wanted to die, there and then.

'You've left me no choice but to kill you,' he said, with a hint of regret.

13

ORDER AND DISORDER

1

Eighteen years earlier

Gare du Nord: Major Crime officer saves woman from Metro attackers

6 October 2003
Le Parisien – in association with AFP

On Friday evening, Mathias Taillefer, a plain-clothes officer from the Major Crime Unit, leapt in to protect a woman from a knife attack on Line 4 of the Paris Metro.

Three youths in their late teens had boarded the underground service bound for Gare de l'Est just after 10 p.m. During the journey, they tried to rob a female passenger who was sitting in the carriage by holding a knife to her throat and another between her legs. Upon witnessing the incident, the Major Crime captain, who was travelling home after his shift, approached the attackers to ask them to stop. When one of the young men responded by punching him in the chest, the officer took out his badge and revealed his identity – a move which only inflamed the situation. As one of the youths raised his knife to stab the woman, Captain Taillefer stepped in to shield the civilian and sustained violent stab wounds to his abdomen, hands and arms.

On arrival at the Gare de l'Est, the three attackers immediately left the train. Despite his injuries, the officer managed to draw his service gun and crawl onto the platform to fire at one of the attackers, who was hit in the spine. His two accomplices were able to flee the scene.

Mathias Taillefer was transferred to Saint-Antoine Hospital. His condition is not believed to be life-threatening. The youth who was shot is alleged to be a seventeen-year-old minor already known to the police. He was taken to Bichat Hospital in a critical condition.

The head of the Paris Police Prefecture, who rushed straight to the scene, has refused to comment until the Paris transport network CCTV footage has been analysed and the force has conducted an internal enquiry. Meanwhile, the young woman targeted in the attack, Alice Bakker, was quick to pay tribute to her rescuer: *'That officer saved my life. He was the only person on board who came to help. By stepping in to shield me, he took the blows that were meant for me. I can never thank him enough, and I hope his injuries aren't too serious.'*

Altercation on Line 4: Officer placed under formal investigation

10 October 2003
Le Parisien – in association with AFP

Mathias Taillefer, the Major Crime Unit captain who saved a young woman from a knife attack on the Paris Metro (see edition of 6 October), has been put under formal investigation for '*wilful aggravated violence by a person invested with public authority*'. He is accused of having opened fire on a seventeen-year-old boy from Roissy-en-Brie, Elias Abbes, after the latter had stabbed him repeatedly. Taillefer has been placed under supervision pending trial and suspended from all police duties, the Paris prosecutor announced.

After suffering serious injuries to his chest and arms, the officer had been admitted to Saint-Antoine Hospital and was therefore not in a fit state to be questioned sooner. During his police interview, he maintained that he had opened fire '*to prevent extremely dangerous individuals from inflicting harm*'.

While Taillefer's solicitor declined to comment at this stage of the investigation, police unions have reacted strongly. In a joint statement, Alliance and UNSA Police described his indictment as '*scandalous and irresponsible*', warning that, '*Heaping opprobrium on police officers* will do nothing to improve the safety of our citizens.'

Alice Bakker, the young woman Taillefer protected from being stabbed, said that she was '*disgusted*' by the decision. '*I visited him in hospital as soon as I could to pledge my support and to thank him for saving my life. This man's a hero, and it's sickening how his actions are being turned on their head.*'

There has been a different take from the camp of Elias Abbes, who was also rushed to hospital in a critical condition after being shot in the lower back. '*Elias is a good boy who didn't pose any threat,*' commented Julia Carles, the lawyer acting on behalf of the family. '*There was no justification for shooting at him like an animal.*' She also refused to condemn the violent unrest that has rocked Roissy-en-Brie in recent days. A protest march departing from the town square has been organised for this weekend, and a solidarity fund has been set up in support of the Abbes family.

14

BROKEN HEART SYNDROME

1

Paris Police Prefecture Annex
2 February 2007

Dr Boisseau: Good morning, Captain Taillefer.

Mathias Taillefer: Good morning.

Boisseau: Please, take a seat. Do you know what my job is?

Taillefer *(sitting down at the other side of the desk)*: Erm, you're a shrink.

Boisseau: I prefer 'psychiatrist'. As you know, administrative proceedings are still ongoing to decide on your reinstatement to your duties. My role today is to provide an opinion on whether you're ready to resume your post in the Major Crime Unit. Do you understand?

Taillefer: It's within my grasp so far, yeah.

Boisseau: I'll be straight with you: my opinion is purely advisory. I don't have the final say on anything.

(Mathias looks at his watch and opens his leather jacket without taking it off, ready to leave if things go badly.)

Boisseau: I've read your file carefully. It's now over three years since the incident. What's your vision on it today?

Taillefer: My 'vision'? I was stabbed to the bone six times! Want to see the scars? Do you reckon you can stomach the *vision*?

Boisseau: There's no point getting aggressive. I'm here to help you.

Taillefer: I don't think so.

Boisseau (*twiddling a pen*): What I'm keen to establish is your outlook on the victim today.

Taillefer: The victim? You mean the woman who was attacked, Alice Bakker? I don't know. I haven't heard from her in a long time.

Boisseau: No, the *other* victim.

Taillefer: The other victim was me.

Boisseau (*shaking his head*): I'm referring to the victim you attacked.

Taillefer: Are you joking?

Boisseau (*peering at his notes*): Elias Abbes. He was seventeen years old at the time of the incident . . .

Taillefer: . . . and already with a criminal record as long as his arm.

Boisseau: He was hit by a bullet fired from your service weapon, causing a serious lesion of the spinal cord and irreversible paraplegia. Because of you, the boy will spend the rest of his life in a wheelchair.

Taillefer (*crossing his arms*): You're turning things on their head.

Boisseau: You don't seem particularly moved by what happened to him.

Taillefer: Less than you, that's for sure.

Boisseau: Listen, Captain, I've read the general inspectorate's report and . . . how can I put this? There really are some aspects of the case that I find troubling.

Taillefer: Such as?

Boisseau: How it all started, for one thing. You've just finished work for the week. You're heading home, it's past ten in the evening. You're on the metro and you witness an unremarkable theft.

Taillefer: Unremarkable? With knives?!

Boisseau: A phone theft. There are more than a million every year. Why did you feel compelled to intervene?

Taillefer: It's my job, dammit!

Boisseau: You weren't on duty.

Taillefer: A cop's always on duty. What would you rather I'd done? Let the woman get attacked?

Boisseau: If you hadn't intervened, the boy wouldn't be in a wheelchair today.

Taillefer (*pushing back his chair to stand up*): You know what? I think we can leave it there.

Boisseau: And *I* think you wanted to play the hero.

Taillefer: You don't know what you're talking about. Watch the security footage.

Boisseau: Oh, but I have seen it. That's precisely the point. You stepped in to take the blows instead of the young woman, Alice Bakker, that much I can understand. But then . . .

Taillefer: Then?

Boisseau: When you arrived at the Gare de l'Est, the young men quickly left the carriage. There was no longer any immediate danger, yet in spite of your injuries, you crawled after them and opened fire.

Taillefer: And . . . ?

Boisseau: It's a striking image, wouldn't you agree? You're pouring with blood, seriously wounded, but somehow you haul yourself along the platform and find the strength to get up and shoot the boy in the back . . .

Taillefer: You really do have a nerve.

150

Boisseau *(insistently)*: It's Friday evening, the platform is packed, yet you take the risk of firing anyway. In the middle of the Gare de l'Est, right in the thick of the weekend rush. You could have hit a bystander. It's a miracle no one was killed.

(Mathias exhales deeply, straining to keep his cool. He stares out of the window, looking for a sliver of sky, a ray of sunlight, anything to cling onto.)

Boisseau: Let me tell you my rationale. I have a fifteen-year-old daughter. She takes the metro every Friday night back to her mother's house. She could have been on the platform that evening, and I wouldn't have wanted her to bump into someone like you.

Taillefer: I prevented an attacker from inflicting further harm. I didn't kill or injure any innocent passengers. Don't go thinking I'm about to apologise for anything. If I had my time over, I'd do exactly the same.

Boisseau *(raising his voice to reveal a subtle south-western twang)*: That's a scandalous thing to say!

Taillefer: Elias Abbes, the individual you insist on calling 'the boy'—

Boisseau: He was a boy, for God's sake! He was seventeen!

Taillefer: He's a criminal. You'd know that if you'd bothered looking at his file. Luckily, other people did.

Boisseau: Petty theft doesn't deserve a bullet in the spine!

Taillefer: Abbes wasn't just a thief. Six months earlier, on La Renardière estate in Roissy-en-Brie, he'd stabbed his flick knife up a girl's vagina. A real treasure, your 'boy'!

Boisseau: But when you shot him, you didn't know any of that.

Taillefer: I knew he'd assaulted a woman right in front of me. I knew he was armed, on the run and extremely dangerous.

Boisseau: And to your mind, those are grounds for taking a man's life?

Taillefer: Are you doing this on purpose?

2

Boisseau (*jabbing his pen at the cop*): I'm going to ask you the question one last time, and I suggest you answer without getting clever: why did you shoot Elias Abbes?

Taillefer: I've already told you. What exactly do you want from me?

Boisseau: At the very least, that you show some remorse for your actions. That would help us move forward. That would help *you* to move forward.

Taillefer: Get fucked.

Boisseau: I'll tell you why you opened fire: you couldn't resist. You got too big for your boots, too drunk on your own power. You fancied yourself as some kind of urban Robin Hood, Paris's answer to Charles Bronson. You thought you could play God, Captain Taillefer.

Taillefer: Is that everything? Are we done here?

Boisseau: Not quite, no. I'd like us to talk about Alice Bakker. A press report claims you had a relationship with her.

Taillefer: You mean the column on some woke blog that the Elias Abbes fan club and their lefty lawyer have been touting around to discredit me?

Boisseau: That may be the case. But it's still true, isn't it?

Taillefer: After the attack, Alice Bakker came to visit me in hospital to thank me. We became friendly and had a very brief fling that lasted four or five weeks.

Boisseau: So you exploited your position to seduce a victim?

Taillefer: Are you asking for a punch in the face? Alice Bakker was as lost as me after the attack.

Boisseau: You were 'lost', then? That's a big word.

Taillefer: You might be a shrink, but you have no idea what it's like to live through something like that. Yes, I was lost: as a result of the stab wounds to my stomach, I found out I had a pre-existing health condition.

Boisseau: Which was . . . ?

Taillefer: When they took me to hospital after the attack, a CT scan showed that my heart was inflamed, even though there were no signs of blood in the pericardium. I was told I had a cardiomyopathy that will curse me for the rest of my life.

Boisseau: So ultimately, if you'd never crossed paths with Elias Abbes, they'd never have detected the disease at such an early stage . . .

Taillefer: Think you're smart, do you?

Boisseau: It's an observation of fact. I have to warn you, my report won't be favourable.

Taillefer: No kidding.

(He stands up to leave.)

Taillefer: I forgot to ask: what's she called?

Boisseau: Who?

Taillefer: Your daughter.

Boisseau: Constance, but I don't see what—

Taillefer: If it had been your daughter who'd been attacked in the carriage, I think she'd have been very grateful to have someone like me around. Just remember that while you're writing your report . . .

3

Psychiatric consultation clinic
Place Henri-Bergson — 8th arrondissement, Paris
6 November 2021

Dr Anne Bartoletti: Good afternoon, Mr Taillefer. *(The doctor is a very young psychiatrist, not yet out of her twenties.)*
Mathias Taillefer: Good afternoon.
Bartoletti: Please, make yourself comfortable.
(Taillefer collapses onto the chair. He's jittery, exhausted, wild-eyed, like he's carrying the weight of the world on his shoulders.)
Bartoletti *(consulting her screen)*: You made an appointment for last month and for the month before that, but you never came.
Taillefer: It's true. I'm sorry.
Bartoletti: So, why have you come today?
Taillefer: I don't think I have a choice anymore. It's do or die.
Bartoletti: Why have you left it so long to ask for help?
Taillefer: Let's just say I've had a bad experience with shrinks.
Bartoletti: Have you seen many?
Taillefer: Two or three, but that's enough.
Bartoletti: I understand. Unfortunately, there are

a lot of idiots in my profession.

Taillefer: In mine too.

(A long silence ensues. Taillefer buries his head in his hands, breathing loudly.)

Bartoletti: Tell me, what's the problem?

Taillefer: It . . . It hurts. All the time, day and night.

Bartoletti: What hurts?

Taillefer: Everything. I . . .

(He springs to his feet and zips up his jacket.)

Taillefer: Listen, this isn't going to work. I can't do this – sit here, spill out my life story. I'm not ready.

Bartoletti: You just told me you didn't have the choice. 'It's do or die,' you said. So you clearly are ready. If you don't try now, you never will.

Taillefer: No, I'll never be ready. Just give me some meds to tide me over. Something to make me sleep, forget, switch off. Yeah, that's what I want. To pull the plug – just to lie there, senseless, in the dark.

Bartoletti: I'll write you a prescription, but we can still chat for five minutes, can't we?

Taillefer: No, not here, I'm suffocating, I . . .

(Anne Bartoletti gets up from her desk and walks over to the window. Outside, Square Marcel Pagnol is bathed in sunshine for the first time in ten days and seems to be waiting with open arms.)

Bartoletti: Let's go down to the square, it's a beautiful day.

4

Square Marcel Pagnol
12 Rue de Laborde

(*Holding a can of Coke Zero, Mathias Taillefer is perched on the backrest of one of the few Davioud benches to have escaped the city council's cull. He feels calmer now, soothed by the fresh air. He watches the light playing off the sycamores and horse chestnuts, enjoying the trees' schoolyard familiarity as he continues his tale.*)

Mathias Taillefer: It happened to me when I was least expecting it. As I've explained, it's been a bumpy ride. After the Line 4 incident, I'd fought my way back to being reinstated in Major Crime, but then five years ago, I suffered major heart failure and at that point . . .

Anne Bartoletti: You had to accept that you needed a transplant to survive.

Taillefer: Yes – and it was no picnic finding a match, but again, I battled through. Those months after the transplant were appalling. Because of my health issues, they'd managed to freeze me out of Major Crime, so I decided to quit the force altogether rather than being put out to grass. It was a knee-jerk reaction, and it ended up being a bitter pill to swallow. I guess I felt like I'd lost my place in the world . . .

(*Taillefer breaks off to light a cigarette. The shrink opens her mouth to dissuade him, then changes her mind.*)

Taillefer: I was stagnating. Each day blurred into the next. I couldn't get excited about anything. I read a bit, went to PSG matches, tried to make the most of Paris's cultural scene, but retirement at forty-two just wasn't for me.

Bartoletti: And that's when you met this woman . . .

Taillefer: Yes, in the Grand Palais, at FIAC - the contemporary art fair. Her name was Lena Haddad. She was thirty-eight at the time. A Lebanese-American working for a gallery in San Francisco, who'd travelled to Paris for the fair.

Bartoletti: Did you fall in love immediately?

Taillefer: Yeah. And that had never happened to me before. Everything was transformed. I liked who I was with Lena. My whole being felt revitalised - as if some-one had planted a garden inside me. When someone loves you, life takes on a different fla-vour, a new consistency. When someone loves you, it's like a retrospective justification of all the time you've spent flailing around, all the crap life has thrown at you.

Bartoletti: And did she feel the same?

Taillefer: To begin with, absolutely! We spent three months living together in Paris. She'd made it clear from the outset that she was mar-ried, but that everything was over with her husband.

Bartoletti: And then?

Taillefer: One day, just like that, she announced that she couldn't carry on. It was the twenty-eighth of December, 2017. As soon as she woke up that morning, she told me she still loved her husband. That by behaving as she was, she wasn't being fair to either of us.

Bartoletti: And you didn't see anything coming? No warning signs?

Taillefer: I must have been naïve, but no. The same day, she booked her plane ticket back to San Francisco. I went with her to Charles de Gaulle in a total daze. Then, just before we said goodbye at the gate, she asked me something I found utterly baffling.

Bartoletti *(biting her nails)*: What was it?

Taillefer: She asked me to meet her. Exactly a year to the day later, in our favourite Italian restaurant. In the interim, not a peep – no calls, emails, messages.

(The cop pauses, flicking his gaze to a pair of blackbirds that are squabbling on the grass under a silver maple.)

Taillefer: The separation drove me into a black hole. I didn't know where I fitted anymore. I'd lost the version of myself she'd allowed me to see – that person who, for the first time in my life, I'd felt at peace with.

Bartoletti: What about the meeting?

Taillefer: I turned up the first year – 28 December 2018. Lena was waiting for me at our table in the Number 6. I built my hopes up again. We spent two days together, but then she left like the first time, with the promise that until her dying day, she'd come back to Paris every 28 December.

Bartoletti: It's not easy, but at least she didn't shut down all channels of communication. She's kept open that point of contact between you – it might not be much, granted, but it's tangible.

Taillefer: In December 2019, I couldn't face returning to the restaurant. The day before, I wrote a letter that I left with the waiter, explaining to Lena that I couldn't keep living like that, and that I wouldn't be coming to the meetings anymore.

Bartoletti: Did you keep your word?

Taillefer: Last year there were no two ways about it, with everywhere being closed because of lockdown.

Bartoletti: And this year?

Taillefer: No, I don't want to do it anymore. I feel like I can't move on with my life. I wish I could just crack open my skull and rip out the memory of Lena.

Bartoletti: I wouldn't recommend that – very painful.

(Taillefer can't help smiling as the nearby church clock strikes four, drowning out the gentle murmur of the fountain.)

Bartoletti: Listen, Mathias, what you're experiencing is the age-old game of love – it gives you everything, and it can just as easily snatch it all away. That's what we expose ourselves to, when we take the risk of falling in love.

Taillefer: And you're going to charge me 100 euros for telling me that love's a cruel game?

Bartoletti: No, I'm going to charge you 200 for telling you that I know there's something else.

Taillefer: Something else?

Bartoletti: Something else that's consuming you. Something else you don't want to mention, but that explains the state you're in.

Taillefer: You know what, doc? I think we'll leave it there for today.

15

THE MAN IN THE RED COAT

1

Louise awoke to find herself bound from head to toe, sitting on a metal chair in Mathias Taillefer's living room. The space was unheated, and despite the late-afternoon sun, it was bitingly cold. It took the young woman several minutes to come to her senses completely. Her heart was hammering, the back of her skull felt like it was about to explode, and her neck was ablaze with shooting pain. A gag had been forced deep into her mouth, preventing her from screaming or breathing normally.

A living nightmare.

Her ankles were fettered together, both hands immobilised behind her back with nylon cable ties. When she realised the true scale of her predicament, Louise's heart began to thrash even faster, its frantic march pulsing in her temples as she trembled and sobbed. Who was this guy? What the hell had she got herself caught up in? She might still be alive, but for how long?

Desperately, she tried to turn around, but the cables resisted her every movement. It was then that she heard footsteps approaching, and Taillefer's towering frame appeared before her. With his gun in his right hand.

He no longer resembled the man she recognised. Wild hair, glazed stare, inscrutable features. She tried to catch his eye, but the cop had become a stranger.

Taillefer snapped shut the chamber of his semi-automatic and pointed the barrel at the young woman's forehead. Louise felt her breath freeze in terror. Suddenly her brain couldn't rationalise what was happening. She wanted to cry out, but her screams refused to leave her throat. Yet she couldn't let herself die like this! Without an explanation, without understanding any of what was going on, without knowing why she was there . . .

2

With his finger poised on the trigger, Mathias Taillefer could feel his nerve failing him. *For crying out fucking loud.*

Nevertheless, it wasn't as if he hadn't sensed it. From the first minute, he'd known the girl would be trouble. From their first words, he'd been unsettled by Louise Collange. By her repartee, her doggedness, the spark of intelligence he'd glimpsed in her eyes. Why, ignoring every precaution in the book, had he given her the chance to get a foothold in his life?

Why had he dropped his guard so easily?

Maybe because she hadn't left him the choice.

He fixed his eyes on hers. He saw panic, terror, incomprehension. But what option did he have, now that he'd crossed the point of no return? Now that he'd lost all hope of things blowing over. Now that only the worst solutions remained.

He lowered the gun and Louise's gag.

Buying himself a little more time.

Putting off the moment of reckoning.

The coward's way out . . .

As he'd expected, the girl began to shriek.

'That's it, kid,' he coaxed. 'Knock yourself out, get it all off your chest.'

She let out a long howl, a primal cry to expel her fear, to drive away the whisper of death that had come so close to claiming her.

'But I'd best warn you now: with the double-glazing in here, you can scream as much as you like, but no one'll hear you.'

After the screaming, a fretful silence. Then the question:

'Why . . . Why are you doing this?'

'How many times did I tell you to leave me in peace?' he barked, by way of reply.

'. . .'

'How many times did I tell you I wasn't a good person?'

As he spoke, Taillefer paced in a small circle around the chair to which Louise was tied, his manner becoming more and more aggressive.

'Didn't I tell you it was dangerous to stay with me?'

'. . .'

The ex-cop slammed his fist on the wall.

'DIDN'T I TELL YOU? ANSWER ME!'

'Yes,' she conceded. 'But—'

'There are no buts about it! I warned you.'

Louise's throat was so dry that even without the gag, she

was struggling to breathe. Beads of sweat were trickling from her nape to the base of her spine.

'I wanted to find my mum's killer. I've a right to know how she died.'

'Shut it.'

'Who are you, Taillefer? Who are you really?'

Louise sensed that her aggressor could turn on her at any moment. Her window of opportunity was slim. She needed to regain her composure, regulate her breathing, while at the same time daring to push ahead.

'What's going on, Mathias? Why are you doing this? Explain it to me!'

'There's nothing to explain.'

'That's a cop-out, and you know it. I've done nothing to deserve a bullet in the head.'

'You've been too interfering.'

'That's not an answer. I want the truth – you owe me that much.'

'I don't owe you anything, goddammit! You're a seventeen-year-old kid who should be in her bedroom, at her parents' house, revising for her exams!'

'Untie me! Let me go, Mathias!'

'Stop talking!'

'Think you're the big man because you've got a gun?'

'It helps, yeah.'

Louise hurled down her trump card.

'Untie me, if you want to know what I found out about the woman you believe to be Lena Haddad.'

Lena Haddad?

Silence. At first Taillefer thought he'd misheard, then his brow furrowed. That was all he needed. Why had the

163

Lebanese woman suddenly burst into the conversation? It took him a long moment to string the threads back together.

'You told me she hadn't come to the restaurant.'

'Yeah, well. I lied. Like *you* lied to me.'

'You think I'm falling for a cheap trick like that!'

'It isn't a trick. Lena Haddad isn't her real name either. She's not American, and she doesn't live in San Francisco. But all of that passed you by, too. You obviously weren't such a great cop after all – no wonder Major Crime gave you the boot.'

Taillefer felt his eardrums pulsating and a blistering surge of bile in his stomach.

'Tell me what you found out.'

'Not until you untie me.'

He didn't like taking orders. Once more he trained his SP 2022 on the young woman.

'I won't say it again.'

But this time, Louise stared defiantly back at him.

'Let's not kid ourselves that you're going to shoot, Mathias.'

In his rage, his breathing was almost a growl. He made a superhuman effort to contain his fury.

'You'd already have done it, if you really meant to.'

'Tell me what you know!' he roared, striking Louise's forehead with the barrel of the gun.

But the young woman remained defiant, and Taillefer felt his strength drain from him. She was right: he wouldn't kill her. He was done with all that. Suddenly emptied of his anger, he untied the cables without meeting her gaze.

'Talk. Now!'

'You first,' she demanded, rubbing her stinging wrists. 'Why did you try to stop me going to the police?'

'You've no idea what you're dealing with, little girl.'

Louise pushed her sweat-drenched hair out of her face.

'Two minutes ago you wanted to put a bullet through my head. I don't see what can be worse than that!'

'One day, you might be begging someone to pull the trigger,' Taillefer replied, wearily giving up the fight. *She wants to know . . . Well, let her then . . .*

Except that even he didn't really know where to start.

3

By now the sun was sinking in the sky, bathing the room in a fetching golden glow as the low rays reflected off the glossy slats of the parquet. After slumping into his old Wishbone chair, the only one that didn't cripple his back, Taillefer had begun to unburden his secret.

'A few years ago, after my heart transplant, I was put on the scrapheap at work and wound up leaving the police altogether. I was forty-two years old, and already my body was in tatters. Overnight I found myself out of a job, with no family or any true social connections.'

For a silent type like him, talking didn't come easily; but once the floodgates were open, it had a powerfully liberating effect.

'Around the same time, I started seeing Lena Haddad, but the end of the relationship broke me. I was in a dark place – a very dark place. I'd never have imagined it was possible to feel so utterly alone.'

Titus the friendly-faced beagle had appeared in the room, and, oblivious to the unfolding drama, he eagerly trotted between them, hoping to have his ears ruffled.

'Right when I was at my lowest ebb, I was contacted by a man who'd been my instructor during my military service in Rochefort. He was called Henri Pheulpin, but he'd since adopted the name of "the Man in the Red Coat".'

'"The Man in the Red Coat"?'

'After the executioner in *The Three Musketeers*.'

A memory flashed into Louise's mind.

'When I went with you to the Big Wheel in Place de la Concorde, I saw you talking with a man wearing a red parka!'

'That was him. Anyway, by then Henri Pheulpin had left the army. Based on everything he knew about my career and my personal life, he decided I was trustworthy enough to tell me the story of the Iridium group.'

Louise was now perched on the edge of the coffee table, cupping a glass of water next to Bernar Venet's entwined bronze spirals.

'When you first hear it, the whole thing has a surreal baroque ring to it,' Taillefer acknowledged. 'Like some kind of urban legend or the crap that's spouted on conspiracy theory forums.'

'The Iridium group, you mean?'

'Yes. In simple terms, it's an alliance of a hundred or so elite European and American families who, in the early nineties, decided wherever possible to stop using standard legal channels to settle their private affairs.'

'Why?'

'Some of them thought the system had grown too lenient and half-baked, derailed by far-left ideology and "excuse culture". Others found it too intrusive and wanted to escape the media spotlight.'

Louise blinked several times, slightly discombobulated. The cop's explanation was taking a bewildering turn, a million miles from her mother's death. Taillefer pressed on.

'Their desire for their own justice system was inspired by the idea of an "honour court". Does the term mean anything to you?'

She rubbed her eyes to spur her memory, but nothing came.

'Not really.'

Taillefer dug in his shirt pocket for his lighter and cigarette pack, then lit one.

'The honour court was a special legal body established in France by Henry IV at the start of the seventeenth century. At the time, the idea was to put an end to the duels that were decimating the aristocracy.'

Grimacing, he spat out a thick cloud of smoke, as if the tobacco had scorched his throat.

'The court could only be convened by the nobility, to deal with disputes where "honour" was at stake.'

'Who ruled on the cases, back then?'

'The Marshals of France – the highest-ranking army generals, who mostly came from big-name aristocratic families.'

'So that's the principle the hundred families revived?' Louise asked, after a moment's reflection. 'You're saying that right now, there's a special court they can use if they feel their honour's been tarnished?'

'Got it in one.'

Taillefer squinted against the brightness. There was something captivating about the late-afternoon sun as it danced

off the contours of the bronze sculpture, tracing out a hyp-
notic tunnel of light. A shaft of honeyed gold.

'The sentences delivered by the court are fast, final and
immediately enforceable,' he explained.

'But who enforces them? The Man in the Red Coat?'

'Henri Pheulpin is the strong arm of the group, yes. Sometimes he performs the orders himself, but usually he calls on
a small number of trusted henchmen.'

'And you're one of the henchmen, Mathias, right? You're
a killer?'

He winced at the term.

'I've accepted a few contracts,' he admitted, almost apolo-
getically. 'Partly because I couldn't give a royal shit about
anything – especially not so-called morality – and partly
because it's extremely well paid. The principle's the same
every time: you're given a first name, a surname and a photo.
Then the rest is up to you. You have a week to complete the
job and eliminate the target. All the details are communi-
cated in person, during a single meeting. It's all done the
old-school way – no phones, no internet, no explanations.
Nothing that can be traced. You don't get to know the reasons for the sentence or the parties involved.'

'So that day, in Place de la Concorde, the Man in the Red
Coat told you to kill someone. Is that right?'

He nodded.

'Me?'

'No.'

'Then who?'

'Angélique Charvet.'

'Why?'

Taillefer pulled a face.

'I've given it a lot of thought. My theory is that the Sabatinis are part of the hundred families, and that Angélique tried to screw them over in some way. Your mum, being quick on the uptake and always after easy money, must have seen an opportunity and tried to blackmail her. So Angélique got rid of her.'

Louise let a long silence go by.

For the first time, she saw the scene in all its horror. The nurse hurling Stella over the balcony rail. The brutality of her mother's death. And the image was unbearable; a dagger through her flesh.

'I'm going to help you find Angélique Charvet,' she declared.

A fresh silence fell.

'I'm going to help you find her. And I'm the one who's going to kill her.'

She rose from the coffee table, her mind seemingly made up. Taillefer rushed to talk her down.

'You have to forget this whole thing. The implications are too big for you to understand – too big for me, even. You're not . . .'

Realising she'd vanished from view, he turned his head to look for her. When she reappeared, she was armed with the Venet bronze.

Taillefer saw the sculpture flying towards his face at supersonic speed. He didn't even have time to raise his hands to shield himself.

16

THE DARK NIGHT
OF THE SOUL

1

Fuck . . .

Hook, line and sinker.

Taillefer had swallowed the bait like a baby. The bronze sculpture that she'd slammed into his face had nearly taken his eye out. In any case, it had left him punch-drunk for a long time, and the little bitch had seized on his state to tie *him* to the chair in turn. He let out a howl of rage, struggling with all his might to break free. But Louise had strapped the cables as tightly as they'd go, and the girl sure knew how to tie a knot.

Returned to sender.

The shame of it.

His brow had been spewing blood, and he could feel the crusted trails cracking on his face. How long had he been knocked out? It was pitch black, but in winter that didn't offer much clue as to the time of day or night. From a distance, he could hear Titus barking. Louise must have locked the animal upstairs before making herself scarce.

He gave a fresh roar of rage, hit by the urge to smash everything around him.

Forcing himself to focus, he tried to assess the situation. Things were as bad as they could get. Where was Louise now? What was she planning? To alert the police? To go after Angélique Charvet herself? Taillefer had ballsed up twice over. The honour court could be exposed to the world because of him. In the best-case scenario, he'd spend the rest of his days in prison. In the worst, he'd snuff it here like a dog.

He *had* to try something. Bearing down with all his weight, he managed to tip the chair so that it fell onto its side. There was a sickening crack as his shoulder hit the floor. Gritting his teeth, he attempted to crawl across the parquet, but was unable to make it very far. He steeled himself again. Wasn't it in the most fiendish of circumstances that the human mind was at its most ingenious? Although on this occasion . . .

He closed his eyes.

Despite all his woes, one thought burned insistently in his mind: Lena had turned up for the meeting. He found it hard to believe. Perhaps Louise had taken him for a ride? The pain of that failed love affair still tormented him. He was haunted by questions without clear answers, as though some crucial detail had escaped him. He didn't want to get carried away, but if Louise had been telling the truth, at least Lena hadn't forgotten, at least she hadn't drawn a line under their relationship. Right now, that was the only speck of hope he could cling to.

As for the rest . . .

He suddenly realised why his thighs were cold: he'd pissed

himself. The ultimate humiliation. At the indignity of it, he started bawling like a kid. He was going to die there, lying in his own piss and shit. What a sordid way to go. He could already picture the epitaph in *Le Parisien*:

Square de Montsouris: Ex-cop found dead trussed up like a chicken in his living room

The news would get a few laughs on social media, then the world would forget all about him. *Fuck . . .* It couldn't end like that.

He thought back to Stella Petrenko. From the start, he'd felt a kind of kinship with the dancer. The way their lives had been defined by disappointment. Their scarred bodies. Their inability to turn the page. Forever doomed to see the coin land the wrong way up. Thwarted by a life that ripped you apart and drowned you under a relentless, unassailable tide of setbacks.

He stayed there for a while longer, lamenting his fate. Crying had always made him feel insanely better, sending his anxiety, fear and anger ratcheting down. Blubbing was a 100-percent natural benzo – proof that every so often, God got things spot-on.

Time stretched on. Through the window, he could see the darkness deepening, without knowing if it was nine o'clock at night or three in the morning. How long had he been lying there? Twenty minutes? An hour? More? For a brief moment, his hopes soared as he saw Titus yapping on the other side of the window.

'Good boy! Good boy!' he called, writhing to catch the beagle's attention.

The beagle must have managed to escape. On noticing his master, he went wild, barking as if his life depended on it. Perhaps a curious neighbour would be lured out to investigate?

But the minutes rolled on, and no one came. The terrace and garden didn't face onto the street, and there were no houses behind. Taillefer's hopes fell almost as quickly as they'd risen. As time continued to swell around him, his thoughts became rambling, blurred. He might even have drifted off to sleep.

But then a noise shook him from his stupor. The long scraping of a garden chair, followed by the sight of a torch sweeping the terrace. Taillefer jolted to attention. Someone was there!

'Help!' he shouted, praying to make himself heard.

The light momentarily vanished.

Bollocks.

'Help!' he cried again.

A figure appeared behind the patio doors. A male silhouette in a hooded parka that shadowed his face. Taillefer peered hard, but he couldn't make out the visitor's features. The torch swung in the direction of the living room. Its beam lingered on the cop's face. Then the figure seized a chair that he hurled against the glass a first time, then a second. On the third attempt, the pane shattered. Taillefer watched with his heart in his mouth as the silhouette edged closer.

Friend or foe?

Finally the stranger knelt down, giving Taillefer a view of his face.

It was Romuald Leblan.

2

'I suggest you explain what the fuck you're doing here. And you'd better make it convincing.'

It was past 2 a.m. Ten minutes had elapsed since the geek had freed Taillefer from his tethers. The cop had put on a change of clothes, and the two men were now sitting at the kitchen island. Taillefer had made coffee, and Romuald was dabbing at the cop's brow with a cotton pad and antiseptic.

'You could start by thanking me, couldn't you?'

'I'll thank you once I know what the hell's going on. I'm wary of sorts like you.'

'At least I don't go around wetting myself.'

'Maybe not, but according to your mum, you sometimes piss into plastic bottles instead because you're too scared to leave your room to go to the toilet. Not much better, is it?'

'Whatever!'

'And careful with that pad – you're burning my eye out!'

Taillefer had his mojo back. His sense of relief was overwhelming, only intensified by how afraid he'd been before. The old dog wasn't beaten yet. For once fate seemed to be smiling on him, allowing him to play on for another round. But before he celebrated too hard, he needed to understand what was behind the geek's sudden appearance – and find Louise Collange.

'OK, kid. Tell me how you ended up here. I thought you never left your cushy little den.'

Romuald fumbled for words.

'It's just . . . that girl . . .' he began, turning crimson.

'What girl?'

'The blonde girl who came with you to question me. Louise, Stella Petrenko's daughter.'

'Yeah, what about her?'

Romuald stuck a large plaster over Taillefer's unruly brow.

'I'd already seen her from my window, while she was visiting her mum. I thought she was well fit.'

The cop sighed. He was in no mood to play matchmaker for some acne-ridden youth.

'Right, and your point is?' he pressed. 'How does that explain why you're here? Spit it out, for Christ's sake!'

'OK, OK! No need to shout. This morning, just before you left, I slipped one of my AirPods into her rucksack and the other into her coat pocket.'

'What the devil are those?'

'AirPods? They're wireless headphones.'

'Why did you do that?'

'So I could track Louise's location.'

Taillefer was beginning to compute. Inside the earbuds was a tiny Bluetooth chip, which enabled their owner to find them if they were mislaid.

'What the hell were you thinking? Have you got a screw loose? You can't stalk people without their permission. Do you understand that?'

'You should be thankful – that's how I managed to find you. If I hadn't taken the initiative, you'd still be here stewing in your own piss.'

Taillefer toyed with smashing the boy's head against the worktop, but eventually settled for a more educational approach.

'That's no justification. You should at least have a few

175

principles in life – red lines that you don't cross, whatever happens. Got it?'

But the geek wasn't listening. He'd already taken his laptop from his rucksack, connected it to his phone and booted up the Apple geolocation app.

'When I started tracking Louise, I assumed she lived here.'

'No, this is my house,' Taillefer corrected him.

'But after a while, the AirPods began heading in different directions. One of them stayed here, and the other went on the move.'

Taillefer frowned. Something was bothering him. He glanced back at the sofa, and the reason came to him: in her haste, Louise had left without her coat. He went over to grab the parka and found the right earbud in one of the pockets.

'And the other one?' he asked. 'Where did she go next?'

'I think Louise is planning a holiday,' Romuald replied.

'A holiday?'

'The last time I checked, the tracker was somewhere around Orly Airport.'

'Show me.'

On the screen, the left AirPod – probably still in Louise's rucksack – was indicated on the map by a small circle hovering over the suburbs south of Paris. When Romuald zoomed in, the sprawl of Orly's four terminals came into view, but as he enlarged the map further, they saw that the circle was just outside the airport – specifically, at the Mercure hotel.

Taillefer was reassured by the finding. Very few planes took off in the middle of the night. Louise must have wanted to make a quick getaway, but the Covid situation had led to a skeleton flight schedule and was playing havoc with international travel. Nevertheless, to book a room so close to the airport, that had to mean she'd found a ticket for the following day. *But to where?*

3

The geek jolted the cop from his thoughts.

'What's your name? You never said.'

'Mathias, but everyone calls me Taillefer.'

'Where does that hail from?' Romuald asked.

'It's the name of a small mountain range in the Alps, in the Isère. My dad's family came from there.'

'Why were you tied to that chair, Mathias?'

The cop eyed the kid for a moment, pondering his unfortunate bowl cut and virginal features.

'It's none of your business and it's too long-winded to explain.'

'If you're not a cop anymore, what do you do?'

'I can't tell you that. It could put your life in danger.'

'That wouldn't be any great loss.'

'Let me stop you there: I'm not your mother, and I'm not about to go snivelling over your fate. I've enough to be dealing with.'

'You're not looking for an apprentice, by any chance?'

'An apprentice?'

'Yeah, a sort of intern. I could do odd jobs for you – like cooking, say. Speaking of which, do you fancy something to eat? I could murder an omelette and a hot chocolate.'

'I'm starving as well,' Taillefer conceded. 'I need to think, and I can't focus on an empty stomach. But let's divvy things up differently. I'll sort the food, while you do some digging on your computer. Deal?'

Taillefer didn't dare admit it, but he felt slightly lost when it came to technology. He was a man of books, not screens and machinery.

Oddly, however, Romuald was quick to dampen his hopes.

'I'd better warn you, it's only my mum who thinks I'm a master hacker. Really, I'm just a noob who sometimes strikes lucky.'

The geek's honesty was disarming, but Taillefer felt sure Romuald was underplaying his skills. He sketched out the broad strokes of the story. He and Louise were trying to find Angélique Charvet, the nurse who'd aroused Romuald's suspicions and who they had good reason to believe had killed Stella Petrenko, and perhaps Marco Sabatini.

As he spoke, Taillefer cracked some eggs into a bowl and started whisking them with a fork.

'Charvet left Paris suddenly three months ago. Find me everything you can about her.'

He tipped the mixture into a frying pan and reached for a couple of slices of bread, which he arranged on top of the eggs. While he waited for them to set, he rooted in the fridge drawer for a bottle of blonde ale.

'Do you know if she has a boyfriend?' Romuald queried, glancing up from his screen.

'Angélique Charvet? No idea. Do some delving, it could be interesting.'

'No, Louise!'

'What the hell's that got to do with this? Focus on what I've asked you. If you want me to give you a shot, show me you're capable of concentrating for more than two minutes!'

Turning the bread, he added some cheese and ham before flipping the slices over each other. While the mixture finished cooking, he cracked open his bottle. He liked his beer ice-cold, and had engineered a special compartment in his fridge to keep it at a temperature close to zero. The magic of the first sip gave him a rush of comfort, but was rapidly replaced by a wave of bone-shaking cold. He pressed his hand to his forehead: it was burning.

Shit, the omelette sandwich!

He dived to remove the pan from the heat and slid Romuald's meal onto a plate.

'Enjoy,' he murmured, presenting the geek with the sandwich and cutlery.

'This looks great, thanks!'

'Are you sure you want a hot chocolate with it?'

'Nah, a beer will do – same as you. Aren't you having anything?'

'Turns out I've lost my appetite. Maybe later.'

'You look knackered.'

'Yeah, I've felt wretched since this morning, and it's been a rough day. Anyway, have you found anything?'

'Potentially. I think Louise might be heading for Italy.'

'Go on.'

'There's not much about Angélique Charvet online, but in the most recent results, look what comes up.'

Romuald swivelled his MacBook so the cop could see.

'I'm pretty sure Louise must have found this,' he continued, 'and that she's bought a ticket to Venice on the back of it.'

Taillefer leant over to peer at the text on the screen.

AcquaAlta Foundation: Frenchwoman Angélique Charvet appointed as Special Advisor
PRESS RELEASE

Following an AcquaAlta Foundation board meeting on 9 December, French national Angélique Charvet has been appointed as a special advisor on the recommendation of Lisandro and Bianca Sabatini.

Miss Charvet's primary responsibility will be overseeing the development and promotion of the Sabatini Collection exhibition space in Venice.

In a statement, Bianca Sabatini expressed her satisfaction at the appointment: 'The board is confident that Angélique Charvet's enthusiasm and generous spirit will lead her to every success in the role.'

Established in 1984, the AcquaAlta Foundation is one of the leading philanthropic organisations in Italy, funding projects centred on the arts, education and female empowerment. The Foundation also boasts one of the country's largest collections of modern and contemporary art.

Miss Charvet will take up her duties on 3 January. The first exhibition under her tenure will be a posthumous retrospective of Marco Sabatini's work entitled 'The Young Man Against the Army of the Dead'.

Romuald was on a roll.

'I did some research: the Sabatinis have a house in Venice, the Veziano palace.'

Taillefer rubbed his eyes. There were a lot of unknowns in

the geek's theory, but it was a lead worth pursuing. He went to retrieve his wallet from the key tray in the hallway.

'Try to book me a ticket to Venice,' he told Romuald, handing him his credit card. 'Leaving from Orly, the earlier the better.'

Leblan typed away at breakneck speed.

'There's an EasyJet flight at seven fifteen, but it's full.'

'And the next one?'

'There are still some seats left on the eight thirty-five.'

'OK, that'll do. Book me something comfortable.'

There ensued a lengthy toing-and-froing to complete the mandatory Covid contact tracing form. The airline also needed a negative PCR test from the past forty-eight hours, but the geek assured Taillefer he could easily fake one.

'You're not looking great, if you don't mind me saying.'

'Just do your best,' Taillefer grunted.

'There's something I want to investigate a bit more: I saw that Angélique Charvet has an email address on the AcquaAlta server. I'd like to recover her password if it's not too complicated, but it might take a while.'

'OK, kid, make yourself at home. And since you're being my assistant, come and look in on Titus tomorrow if I'm not back yet.'

While the geek beavered on, Taillefer refilled the beagle's feeder in readiness, then slumped back in his armchair for a moment, with his feet crossed on the coffee table. This was more than just tiredness. He could feel his muscles stiffening and shivers creeping up his thighs, arms and the base of his spine, announcing a rising fever. *Just to put the tin lid on things* . . . His susceptibility to fever was his weak point: he knew it, and he feared it. When it struck, the effects could wipe him out for days. The shivers grew more intense. He gritted his teeth to stop them chattering, tugging up the blanket over his legs to cover his stomach and chest. His pulse was racing nineteen to the dozen. It was the body's age-old defence mechanism, yet in him, for as long as he could remember, it had always taken on alarming proportions. As his system went to war, he was reduced to a helpless casualty, languishing for days on a desolate battlefield.

His hands were icy. Suddenly rabidly thirsty, he imagined himself drinking from a glacial spring. The water was golden and tasted like apple juice. *Shit, he was hallucinating already!* He closed his eyes, deciding to let himself doze off for ten minutes, a quarter of an hour. Then, he'd take some paracetamol and . . .

Giuseppe Rossi Notary Services   Miss Angélique Charvet
24 Via Magenta   Palazzo Veziano
10128 Turin   1364 Calle Tiepolo
Italy   30125 Venice (VE)
                               Italy

9 December 2021, Turin

Dear Miss Charvet,

I am writing to confirm that your statutory declaration of acknowledgement of parentage request has today been approved by the Family Court of Turin.

This declaration officially recognises, without the need for genetic testing, the late Mr Marco Sabatini as the father of your unborn child.

Mr Sabatini's paternity of the child has been established on the basis of testimonies made by three witnesses and of other supporting documents presented to the court, which collectively provide sufficient evidence of parentage in compliance with the requirements of article 23(b).

I attach to this letter a Declaration of Parentage acknowledging the facts set out above, unless or until evidence emerges to the contrary. This Declaration will be mentioned on the child's birth certificate.

Should you require any further information, please do not hesitate to contact me.

Yours sincerely,
Guiseppe Rossi

17

LENA KHALIL

1

Thursday, 30 December

On hearing the blare of his phone alarm – a frenzied mambo beat that was supremely unsuited to the situation – Mathias Taillefer thought it was a mistake. He didn't feel like he'd slept, yet somehow it was 6 a.m. He attempted to stand but was forced to stop halfway, hampered by his feverish state. His joints had seized up, his skull was pounding and he was trembling from head to toe.

Woozily, he managed to haul himself to the bathroom, but balked at the prospect of showering. Instead, he bundled together his go-to survival kit: max-strength paracetamol, esomeprazole for the heartburn, vasodilators for the blocked nose, plus all his usual transplant patient drugs. With a monumental effort, he got dressed and called a taxi, and didn't even try to stomach a coffee.

Romuald was nowhere to seen, but he'd done a sterling job, leaving an assortment of printouts for Taillefer to find: his boarding pass, a PCR test dated from the previous day, and a letter to Angélique Charvet from an Italian notary that the geek must have unearthed in her inbox. The cop stashed the paperwork and his medication in a leather satchel, then retreated to the sofa to wait for the taxi, sitting with his eyes closed and an ice-filled flannel over his forehead while Titus lolled on his lap.

When the cab arrived, he braved the freezing rain to dive into the back seat and didn't move for the rest of the journey. Between his rigid body and his stupefied brain, he doubted he could make it. He had no more puff to give, nothing left in the tank. But in spite of everything he clung on, straining every nerve, trying to snatch a few minutes' rest before facing the crowds. He'd just have to bite the bullet until the paracetamol kicked in. He had to get on that plane, whatever it took.

Orly. Scarcely any better than Charles de Gaulle, the most soul-destroying of all the major tourist-capital airports. The airport that made you hate Paris before you'd even set foot in the city. Although in Covid times, at least the Paris airport authorities could offer some justification for the ambient chaos – interminable queues, useless information boards, the couldn't-give-a-damn attitude of the staff, the belligerence of the passengers. The relentless feeling of being herded like animals to the slaughter.

But again, Taillefer dug in, going through the motions as mindlessly as possible to conserve the little strength he had. After taking half an hour to get through security, he only just reached the gate in time and was one of the last to board. To his surprise, the flight was far from full. The latest change in travel rules had wrongfooted several passengers, who'd been turned away after failing to produce the necessary documentation. Taillefer wove along the aisle to the eight-eenth row, where he offered a plump retiree his front-row place in exchange for the 'row Z' spot she'd been allocated – a middle seat sandwiched at the arse-end of the plane. The woman jumped at the chance, and Taillefer claimed her place next to Louise, who promptly woke up. When she saw him, the young woman let out a yelp of shock.

With her washed-out face, lank hair, dark circles and bleary eyes, she didn't look much cleverer than him.

'You weren't very nice to me earlier . . .' he began, motion-ing with his index finger to the gash on his brow.

'. . . *On behalf of your cabin crew, I'd like to welcome you aboard this Airbus 320. Boarding is now complete, and we'll be taking off very shortly for Venice Marco Polo Airport . . .*'

'. . . but I don't hold it against you, and I even got up at the crack of dawn this morning to stop you doing something stupid.'

'*Our estimated flight time is one hour and thirty-five minutes. Safety information can be found on the seat in front of you . . .*'

'The two of us had just started having a little chat when we were interrupted. And since we're going to have a while to talk, I'd like to pick up where we left off.'

2

The plane was now coasting above the clouds. As soon as they'd left behind the Paris pollution, the leaden skies had given way to a pillowy mass of pink. It sure was easier to breathe 30,000 feet above human idiocy. The sight of the sun and the effects of the paracetamol had perked up Taillefer,

186

and Louise was feeling brighter too. After a restorative coffee and a madeleine, she'd launched back into her tale.

'On Tuesday evening, like you asked me to, I went to that Italian restaurant near Place de Furstemberg.'

'The Number 6.'

'I was running late. I'd stopped off at home to put on something dressier so they wouldn't think I was underage. When I arrived, Lena still wasn't there. I sat down at the bar, then a few minutes later she walked in. I recognised her straight away. She was just as you'd described her – forty-something, Mediterranean-looking, olive skin, dark hair, pale eyes.'

Taillefer was listening intently, his senses in overdrive, preparing himself for everything . . . and for nothing.

'She went to the bar and told them she had a reservation in the name of Lena Khalil. Not Haddad, Khalil. It wasn't the name you'd given me, so I decided to find out more. And not to say anything to you until I'd got to the bottom of it. I knew it was never a case of something for nothing with you – although at that point, I didn't know just how true that was—'

'Come on, get to the point,' Taillefer pressed.

'She sat down next to me at the bar without noticing me. She was keyed-up, constantly checking her phone and watching the door as people came in. I waited like that for about twenty minutes, not really knowing what to do. Then she got up to go to the toilet, so I grabbed the chance to call you.'

'And then?'

'After that, she came to sit down again and tried to get the barman's attention to order another martini. And that's when I took advantage to . . .'

'. . . To what?'

'I slipped a ten-euro note under my glass of Perrier, then walked out with her phone that she'd put down on the bar.'

'You nicked her phone! Why on earth . . . ?'

'To figure out the mystery, of course! I didn't go very far. I went into a bar in Rue de Buci and found a table. The screen was still unlocked. I scrolled through her photos, read her emails and her notes. She basically had her entire life on her phone. After clicking on a few news links, I was able to piece together the whole story – but it wasn't the one you'd told me.'

'I didn't tell you any story.'

'OK, fair enough. Let's say it wasn't the one Lena had told you, then.'

Taking out her own phone, Louise swiped open the screen and began talking Taillefer through the photos she'd purloined.

'In the early 2010s, Lena Khalil was a thirty-something vet living in Beirut with her husband, Simon Verger, a teacher at the French international school. Simon was originally from Biarritz, and he'd met Lena during an Erasmus exchange in Lebanon.'

Already racked with tension, Tailler was gripping his arm-rest as if he wanted to pulverise it.

'The couple married in 2011. Their eldest son Baptiste was born in 2013, followed by their daughter Anna in 2015. At that point, things couldn't have been more perfect.'

Taillefer had put on his reading glasses, his eyes riveted to the idyllic images on the screen. The vision of happiness hit his stomach like hot acid. Resentment and bitterness were toxic, he knew, but when it came to his relationship with Lena, he was incapable of being the bigger man.

'Everything changed in the summer of 2016,' Louise continued. 'During a family boat trip on the Basque coast, Simon was struck by a jet ski while swimming with their kids. He died on the way to hospital.'

Taillefer winced. He could picture the horror of it, the violent irruption of death without a moment's warning. Lena in bits, their two young children orphaned, the unspeakable injustice of losing their father overnight without ever truly having known him. But why had Lena never told him? Why had she cast her husband as an obstacle to their relationship, when all along he was dead?

'The weeks and months that followed were brutal,' Louise went on. 'Lena couldn't come to terms with what had happened. She stopped working, moved back in with her mum, sank into depression.'

Taillefer felt a stabbing pain in his chest, as if his heart had constricted. He fought to catch his breath, wiping his forehead with his sleeve. It was drenched in sweat. His initial curiosity had been replaced by an urgent need to know. The truth was no longer a holy grail, but a simmering danger, threatening to shatter the flimsy foundations on which he still stood.

'In the end she was admitted for psychiatric treatment, first in Beirut, then at Saint-Anne Hospital in Paris . . .'

Taillefer had the nasty sensation that Louise had planted a bomb under his seat. That a vital detail had somehow passed him by. There had to be *something more*, but he couldn't see what.

'One day,' Louise pressed on, 'while searching online, Lena found an article from *Nice-Matin*. A feature talking about your heart transplant.'

He vaguely remembered the piece. After his operation, he'd spent three weeks in a specialist recovery unit near Vence. He'd been at his lowest ebb, bored shitless, and had let a journalist cajole him into giving an interview for their annual organ donation campaign.

Louise handed him the crumpled article she'd printed from the newspaper's website. He scanned the headline and opening paragraph:

INTERVIEW
Mathias Taillefer, alive and kicking thanks to a new heart
'*I know how lucky I've been,*' admits the police officer, who's currently recovering at the Maison des Cimes after receiving a heart transplant last month.

'In the article, the journalist says you'd been waiting for the transplant for a long time.'

Taillefer's facial muscles tensed.

'I had, but I don't—'

'She says it's because you have a rare blood type, Vel-negative. It's a subject I know about – we did a unit on it earlier this year. Vel-negative is extremely uncommon. Officially there are only 400 people with it in France. If Vel-negative patients are transfused with Vel-positive blood, they develop anti-Vel antibodies that attack and destroy the new blood.'

'Yeah . . . so?' Taillefer stammered. He could feel himself

faltering, like the air had suddenly been knocked out of him.

Louise moved in for the coup de grâce.

'Simon Verger, Lena's husband, was Vel-negative. He was one of the rare people with his blood type to have joined the donor register. And when you look at the date of his accident and the date of your transplant, there's pretty much no doubt – you have his heart.'

Taillefer saw the cabin whirling around him, felt himself sweating, fighting for breath. Piece after piece, the dire jigsaw was slotting into place, revealing the intolerable truth: Lena had decided to find the patient who'd been given her husband's heart. A vision surged from his memory: that way in which, when they were lying together, Lena would rest her head on his chest. She could stay like that for hours on end. But it wasn't Taillefer's heartbeat she was listening to: it was her husband's.

The cop was floored, mortified, assailed by searing emotions: anger, hatred, humiliation, the urge for revenge. The only magical time in his life had been a sham. The only glimpse of happiness he'd known had been an illusion. A trick. A lie.

He clenched his fists. He wanted to smash everything in sight. Then to blast himself to kingdom come.

It wasn't him Lena had loved. He'd just been a conduit for her beyond-the-grave reunion with her husband.

'I honestly think Lena came to love you, Mathias,' Louise insisted, trying to defuse the rage she could see coursing through him. 'But she didn't dare tell you the truth, for fear of how you'd react.'

But Tailler was no longer listening. His mind was boiling over, becoming molten lava. And from the chaos, another image erupted before him: a dagger plunging through his heart, to kill Simon Verger a second time. He wrenched off his mask to stop himself choking, took a gulp of water. A metallic taste formed in his mouth. Salty, ferrous.

The taste of blood.

18

TWO KILLERS IN THE HOUSE

1

Thursday, 30 December
Venice

The gleaming Riva Aquarama eased into the Zattere quayside. After mooring the speedboat, the pilot, one of the
Sabatini family bodyguards, helped Angélique Charvet
down onto the promenade.

The young woman had never felt happier. Today marked
a milestone moment in her new life – her first interview
as Special Advisor to the AcquaAlta Foundation, to pres-
ent the forthcoming exhibition of Marco Sabatini's work.
The meeting with the *Vogue* journalist had been arranged by
Bianca herself, in a restaurant a stone's throw from the Punta
della Dogana. The Sabatini name was an 'open sesame' to
every door. Angélique had spent three months experiencing
the heady proof of it. Clothes, jewellery, trips, professional
opportunities: it seemed to her that suddenly, her wishes
knew no bounds.

As she strolled along the cobbles of the Giudecca, Angélique had the sense of walking through a 1960s postcard. The flowers in the windows, the dazzling silver sunlight bouncing off the Grand Canal and – most strikingly – the rare calm enveloping the city. To its credit, Covid had purged Venice of the tourists and tour operators that usually spewed from the cruise liners to run riot over the place. Catching her reflection in the window of a Venetian mask shop, Angélique liked what she saw. With her new blonde haircut, black dress, cream cashmere coat and irresistible Capucines handbag, she looked radiant, fancy-free. Like Léa Seydoux in a Louis Vuitton ad campaign.

Everyone marvelled at how much pregnancy suited her. Yet the last scan had troubled her – the galloping heartbeat, the crispening outline of the face, the size of the foetus, now almost 20cm long. The due date was closing in. Bianca and Lisandro were in raptures, staying by her side each step of the way. Every bit the dutiful daughter, she'd given them the honour of choosing the name.

Angélique was savouring every moment of her rebirth. She was exactly where she wanted to be. Her new life was sculpted in the image of Venice: noble, elegant, refined. *Serenissima!* At last, she'd found her rightful place. She'd crafted her renaissance without any help from anyone, by the work of her own humble hands and the smattering of brain cells in her head. Not bad for a girl they'd always written off as mad!

At the restaurant, she was greeted with all the deference befitting a Sabatini. The journalist spent the meal lavishing her with compliments, extolling her work, her appearance, her sense of humour, her stilettos. Angélique couldn't get over how quickly people's perceptions had shifted. It was thrilling and depressing in equal measure. Most people had no true opinions or convictions. They just followed the pack, howled with the wolves, blew in the direction of the wind, fell over themselves to copy the crowd for fear of being cast aside. A fickle, characterless herd, forever scurrying to unite in mediocrity.

Once the journalist had gone, Angélique lingered for a moment on the restaurant terrace. A last *ristretto* gazing out at the Giudecca. The setting was spectacular, offering a majestic panorama over the south of the city. From the stilts of the terrace, the tables and chairs seemed to be floating on the water. So close that, after a while, it was enough to make you seasick.

Shielding her eyes, Angélique could make out the distant dome and bell tower of Il Redentore, silhouetted against the silvery-white sky. She'd recently discovered the history of the church, which had been built in the final quarter of the sixteenth century, while the plague was decimating the Venetian population. Powerless to resist its march, the Doge and Senate had pleaded tirelessly for divine intervention to save the city from the epidemic. The church's construction had been the final roll of the dice in their offerings to the Creator.

Angélique looked away. Even through her sunglasses, the marble façade was blinding. She suddenly felt ill, her unfinished coffee churning queasily inside her. She hadn't slept well the previous night, and the exhaustion was starting to take its toll. The little bastard in her stomach hadn't stopped thrashing around. She'd woken at three in the morning, racked with dread and a creeping panic that the foundations of her new life weren't as solid as she'd first thought.

She rubbed her eyes. Her pelvis was throbbing, giving her the horrid sensation that a lotus flower was unfurling in her uterus. Her breasts were so swollen, it felt like the child might burst out at any second and demand instant feeding.

She sighed. Her mood had transformed. She left the restaurant with the bodyguard and retraced her steps to the quayside. As she passed the mask shop window, she tried to glimpse the reflection she'd been so taken with two hours earlier. But that Angélique had gone. She just looked as bloated as a whale, misshapen, lost.

She climbed back into the Aquarama with relief, hoping the ride back to the Sabatini palace would clear her head. *Fresh air, pronto!* As the boat pulled away from the Zattere, she once more spied the ominous silhouette of Il Redentore. She thought back to the building's origins. A desperate plea to the one who'd delivered humanity from its sins. Didn't it always come back to that? The lure of evil, the spectre of fear, and the illusory desire for redemption?

2

The balmy late-morning air was a distant memory. Buffeted by salty gusts, the city had become oppressive, almost hostile. The sky hung in a dense grey mass, fizzing with glints of orange that grew more intense as the Aquarama sliced through the waves of the Grand Canal. The telltale signs of the sirocco, the dusty wind that swept up from the Sahara to cast an apocalyptic atmosphere over the floating city.

As the boat lurched perilously against the headwind, Angélique huddled on the back seat, swaddling herself in her shawl. Feeling a rush of nausea, she asked the bodyguard to slow down.

Everywhere she looked, Venetians were hurriedly erecting temporary walkways, raising the level of the existing street system to keep the city passable despite the impending weather event. Angélique had filed the news in the back of her mind, thinking little of it, but the previous day, the Venice tide forecasting centre had warned of a worrying rise in water levels. The canals were swollen by the heavy autumn rains, and residents in at-risk or low-lying areas had received a text giving them notice to put in place the *paratia*, the metal barriers designed to stop the waters entering through doors and windows. Sirens had rung out across the city, with the four warning tones indicating exceptionally high surges of over 140cm.

The hubbub hadn't fazed Angélique in the slightest. As far as she was concerned, the rising tides were all part of Venice's legend. St Mark's Square and the surrounding streets – the lowest area of the city – flooded on a regular basis. Shopkeepers grumbled, journalists trotted out the same old chestnuts, and tourists donned their wellies and posed for selfies that they posted on Instagram, thinking they were Albert Londres.

After speeding past the Palazzo Grassi and Ca' Rezzonico, the Aquarama turned onto the straight stretch of canal that led to the Rialto. Just shy of 300 yards from the bridge, the boat came to a stop at the private landing stage of the Veziano palace, a sixteenth-century building with a multi-coloured marble façade topped by two discreet obelisks.

While the Sabatini family's Venetian residence couldn't compete in size with its more iconic counterparts, it was a handsome edifice. Constructed over three sturdy storeys, in a blend of Gothic and Renaissance styles, it sported a wide porchway flanked by double windows on the ground floor, with five sets of windows separated by turquoise columns on each of the upper floors. The figure it cut sat perfectly with the image the family wanted to project: solidity, elegance, a grounding in the past that shored up their ability to face the future.

Lisandro had only recently acquired the *palazzo*, which had been in the hands of the same noble Venetian family for centuries. With the backing of the city council, he'd managed to edge out his rival, one of the richest businessmen in Singapore, and had embarked on extensive renovations which had promptly been interrupted by the pandemic.

As soon as she was free of the boat, Angélique dived inside the palace. The hallway was steeped in darkness, lit only by a large cast-iron lantern that hung imposingly from the middle of the ceiling. The building suddenly felt vast and hostile. Where were the butler and the housekeeper? Bianco and Lisandro had left two days ago for their chalet in the Dolomites, where Angélique had been invited to join them the following day to see in the New Year. But why hadn't any of the staff come to greet her?

She tried the switches. None of them were working. She was about to turn back to alert the bodyguard, then remembered he'd set off back up the canal to refuel. With the lift out of action, she took the stairs to the top floor. Due to the ongoing renovations, it was the only habitable part of the building. Everywhere else was swathed in white sheets and protective tarpaulin, and invaded by scaffolding and work lights.

After a laborious trek up the monumental staircase, she finally reached her princess's quarters. She slammed the door behind her and flung off her coat and heels. The bedroom had all the classic trappings of a Venetian palace: high ceiling adorned with romantic frescoes, terrazzo flooring, an oversized mirror, lashings of gold. Through a small, semicircular window, it was possible to glimpse the Grand Canal. Angélique peered out to observe the city. By now rain had begun to fall in sludgy sheets, drowning Venice in an eerie, otherworldly sepia haze.

She removed the rest of her clothes, then bundled on her nightdress and a cashmere cardigan. The room was icy. Why had they turned off the radiators? She tried twisting the cast-iron valve, but it came away in her hands. She could feel herself shivering, maybe even the start of a fever. *That sodding virus?* She took refuge in bed, burrowing under a padded quilt that was as heavy as a dead donkey. It felt like an unknown poison was seizing possession of her body, cankering it from within. She lay there for a long time in a half-stupor, before finally dissolving into sleep.

When she opened her eyes, she was just as agitated as before. She didn't feel as if she'd slept, but a glance at her phone put her right – it was 7 p.m. The room was bathed in darkness. It was clearly the wind that had woken her, blowing open the clumsily shut window. Gusts of a strength she'd rarely known were howling through the night, perhaps powerful enough to carry the house away.

Angélique got up to close the window, then stared out through the rain-lashed glass. Venice was shrouded in a ghostly mist. The waves of the Grand Canal were inky black, but what troubled her most was the water level. The deluge must have started hours ago. With the electricity still down, she struck a match to light the silver candlestick on her bedside table. As its quivering glow spread through the room, a shadow came into view. An immense, sinister silhouette, expanding before her eyes until it swallowed half the room. Nosferatu swooping down on Ellen. Zeus's thunder consuming Semele. The shadow of the devil, coming to claim his dues.

Angélique whipped around and broke into a scream as she saw the man emerge from behind the door. With all her might, she hurled the candlestick at the intruder's face, then fled as fast as her legs would carry her. As she was tearing away from him, a question flashed through her mind: who had uncovered and betrayed her secret?

3

Her name was Angélique Charvet.

From the moment he'd seen her across the floor of the Enfants Terribles, Corentin Lelièvre had known she wasn't like other girls. It was a Tuesday evening in August. It had rained all day, and the bar on Quai de Jemmapes was quieter than usual. She'd come dressed in a green velvet blazer, jeans, a fitted white-and-blue striped shirt and chunky open-toe heels.

Yoo-hoo! He'd waved to attract her attention, and had unmistakeably spotted the way she recoiled. He was under no illusions – he knew his Tinder photos were misleading. Angélique's face had hardened. For a moment, the journalist had thought she was going to walk straight back out, accusing him of product misrepresentation. But in the end, she grudgingly sat down and ordered a lemon drop. Why had she immediately cast such a spell on him? There was something distinctive about her, an offbeat quality, an aura that was hard to put into words. Helped along by the vodka, she'd started to relax. He'd tried to make her laugh, to show himself in his best light, to embroider the description of his work. She'd listened to begin with, but her interest had swiftly waned. She'd zoned out from the conversation, ordered a second cocktail, then a third. She was there without being there. Numbed, drifting, elsewhere.

Lelièvre had got the message loud and clear that she wasn't attracted to him. That Angélique aspired to greater things. Nevertheless, she'd agreed to come back to his flat in Rue Eugène-Varlin, and she hadn't needed asking twice. She'd been drinking, admittedly, but not enough to be drunk. Later, after replaying the evening from every angle, the journalist would conclude that he hadn't taken advantage of her. Angélique was lucid and willing. She'd gone home in the early hours, leaving him with a gnawing hollowness, a void he couldn't explain. The whole day long, she'd consumed his thoughts. He'd tried to see her again, sending message after message, but all were met with silence. He'd persisted regardless, pushing aside his pride, even writing her a letter begging her to give him another chance.

She'd finally deigned to call him one Sunday evening in September, to tell him to stop harassing her and threatening to report him if he didn't. She wanted nothing more to do with him. He had no business hanging around in her life, and he could shove off and take his pathetic looks, two-bit T-shirts, leftie views, tiny dick and receding hairline with him.

Corentin had hung up in shock, reeling from her words. Never had he felt so contemptible, ugly and worthless. He'd spent a long time scrutinising his reflection in the mirror, and was ultimately forced to admit that the hair grafts he'd had done in Istanbul the previous summer hadn't stayed the course.

He did his best to move on and forget the whole sorry tale, which thankfully he hadn't mentioned to anyone. He made it through the autumn unscathed, managing to push the episode from his mind. But in December, the memory of Angélique rushed back at him with a vengeance. The scene was always the same: her entrance into the bar, her nipped-in green jacket, her fiery hair tumbling over her shoulders like a Klimt muse. No, he wasn't over her. He might have kidded himself otherwise, but the nurse continued to haunt him. However deeply she'd humiliated him, he was still infatuated by her. A toxic, all-consuming, spiteful passion.

He put to use the information he'd gleaned from stalking her on social media. Having kept a note of her address, he journeyed out one evening to Aulnay-sous-Bois. The building was deserted. Overcome by curiosity, he smashed two slats of one of the shutters and broke the glass. He knew it was an act of madness that would come back to bite him one day, but he was possessed, obsessed, seized by a kind of frenzy. He needed to penetrate the mystery of Angélique Charvet. The flat was half-empty, but after turning the place upside down, he struck on a positive pregnancy test and the chemist's receipt proving it had been bought three weeks after they'd slept together.

In that moment, and without being sure of what his discovery truly meant, Corentin flipped. He felt conned, engulfed by a rage that made him lose all control. Angélique's mobile number had been reassigned, she'd wiped her social media accounts, and nobody knew where she now lived. For a journalist, there was a case worth investigating. He knew how to sleuth, and his scant workload left him the time to do it. He finally tracked her down in Italy thanks to her appointment by the AcquaAlta Foundation.

The whole story was mind-boggling. What had happened to make Angélique's life take such an improbable turn? On 18 December, after borrowing the money from his mother, Corentin boarded a plane to Venice. He began by prowling around the places he knew to be associated with the Sabatini family. His instinct was right. Eventually, he spied Angélique leaving Palazzo Veziano. He shouted her name, desperately trying to talk to her, but was warned off by a bodyguard who ordered him not to bother a pregnant woman.

This latest snub drove him into a frenzy, sending his rage off the chart. After poring over the reams of material he'd gathered online, he came upon an article in Italian *Vogue* in which Bianca Sabatini, *l'Ingegnere*'s wife, shared her favourite haunts in Venice. One of her top recommendations was Pasticceria Regazzoni, where she liked to enjoy her first coffee of the day whenever she was staying in the floating city.

It was there that Corentin found her, on the morning of 20 December, sitting at the counter with a pastry and a double espresso. He strode over, introduced himself and told her that he had some important information to tell her.

'Information about what?' she asked, her tone sceptical.

'About Angélique Charvet.'

Bianca stared back at him, wary yet intrigued.

Corentin opened his bag.

4

With a wild swipe, Taillefer narrowly deflected the oncoming candlestick, then spun off in pursuit of Angélique as she hurtled down the stairs. He'd come unarmed, planning to improvise on site as he usually did. Overwrought with fever and exhaustion, his pace was closer to a walk than a run, and he wondered by what miracle he was still on his feet.

But the train had been set in motion, and he knew now that he'd see it through to the end.

On reaching the second floor, Angélique tried to give him the slip in the maze of the *palazzo*. Fighting to keep her in sight, Taillefer wove through the old ballroom, the library, then a succession of small reception rooms. Everywhere he turned there were frescoes, marble statues, Murano glass chandeliers, silk wall hangings, wood panelling that still smelled of polish. But because of the ongoing renovation work, their grandeur was smothered under polythene sheets. Exposed wires dangled from the high ceilings, and builders' ladders and sawhorses hampered his progress.

The storm and the vista of the Grand Canal were never far away, each passing plain and stained-glass window offering a portal onto the raging elements. Taillefer could feel his thoughts blurring. Even the paracetamol he'd taken couldn't hold back his mounting fever. In his head, the figures in the frescoes seemed to be coming alive. Cherubs, satyrs, plague doctors in their waxed robes and sinister vulture masks. Having lost Angélique from view, he followed her on instinct, tracking the scent of fear like an animal. On the first floor, a footbridge led him across a small garden to another wing of the building, then a spiral staircase plunged him into the bowels of the palace. Angélique had been here, he was sure of it.

After groping his way down the final few steps, Taillefer arrived in a vaulted room with a lingering smell of orange blossom. Squinting into the gloom, he glimpsed an enormous fireplace, a cast-iron stove, a traditional gas hob and a set of antique copper pans. *The old kitchens* . . . Against the force of the storm, one of the basement windows had given way, and water was gushing over the sandstone floor tiles. Wading through the puddles, he continued unsteadily onwards, almost collided with a beam, when . . .

A flare of lightning streaked across the stone walls, and Angélique Charvet appeared before him like a terrifying, spectral White Lady. Brandishing a long kitchen knife, she lunged at him with a primal roar, intent on stabbing him. Taillefer knew she was dangerous. She'd killed before, and she wouldn't hesitate to kill again.

The first blow hit his shoulder. He accepted it with resignation, having no time to offer the slightest defence. The contact of the blade came almost as a relief, like a salutary bloodletting purging him of his misery. One more nail in the coffin of his clapped-out body, with its morass of pain that he'd never escape. Angélique withdrew the knife and took position again. Part of him had given up already, almost happy to have it over with. Deep down, wasn't that the reason he'd stuck it out this far? What had the whole investigation been, if not a journey into a labyrinth that could only end in his own death?

He remained just as unmoved as the second blow pierced his stomach. He could feel his eyelids drooping. From the start, this was all he'd been waiting for: to make it out of the chaos, so that he could finally be free.

Deliverance, at last!

Even the sound of the blade was pleasurable. The flesh tearing apart like a ruptured abscess, the hot blood spurting out, glad to escape the rotting husk around it. His engine had burnt out a long time ago. He wasn't even sure how he'd made it this far. Nobody would miss him, except maybe his dog.

Through the shadows, he could make out Angélique's rage-contorted face, her wild hair, the Gorgon-like look in her eyes. He was no better than the murderer before him. Their fates were strangely parallel. He too had killed; he too had been forced to grapple with his dark side.

She raised her arm to finish him off.

Knife blows raining down . . . it was the story of his life.

In a flash, he saw those he'd received in the metro carriage eighteen years earlier. The merciless blade of Elias Abbes. His body shielding Alice Bakker. Like an eerie mirror image, the details of the scene became overlaid in his mind with the one he was currently living through. In this revamped version, Angélique Charvet had replaced the delinquent youth, but the plot was the same – except that this time, he had no one to protect. He recalled the scene with fiendish clarity. The greasy, stale stench of the carriage. The jeering faces of the three little thugs as they circled around him. The other sheeplike passengers making no attempt to intervene. Elias Abbes hurling out blows, then his own body as a rampart, a final line of defence to stop the young woman being injured or killed. It was the role he played best – the boxer backed into a corner, taking his opponent's punches before having any chance to fight back. He was one of life's plodders, boasting neither pizzazz nor finesse, just a doggedness and a stubbornness that, in certain circumstances, could spark genuine acts of courage.

As Angélique's knife came down a third time, Taillefer's body buckled and the cop crumpled, head first, onto the floor.

The waters continued to rise, covering him almost completely. By now he was beyond movement, snuffed out, waiting for death to come. But before the shadows carried him away, a final burst of oxygen flooded his brain, reviving a curious memory: the fleeting moment when, under Abbes's blows, he'd turned to look for Alice Bakker. Their eyes had met, and, despite the peril at hand, he'd tried to put on a reassuring face, to let her know that he was going to protect her, that if she just held on for a few seconds more, the nightmare would be over.

He saw the scene with uncanny vividness.

He remembered Alice Bakker's face perfectly. Her gold-rimmed irises, the dimple on her chin, the gentleness of her face, in spite of her terror.

He remembered Alice Bakker perfectly.

That face, those eyes, that dimple.

They were those of Louise Collange.

5

As soon as she saw her pursuer dissolve into the black waters, Angélique dropped the knife and ran for her life. She skidded her way back up the steps, desperate to escape the hellish basement. She was trembling, her heart was pounding harder than it ever had before, but the victory over her adversary gave her fresh hope that all wasn't yet lost. With her stomach in knots, propelled by survival instinct, she continued up to her bedroom and threw on some jeans, trainers and a baggy sweater. She bundled a few possessions into a rucksack, checked she had cash in her purse, then slipped her passport into her pocket.

Where to now?

She still didn't know, but she had to leave Italy. *And fast!*

Keeping her guard up, she stole back down the stairs, crossed the still-deserted hallway and left the *palazzo*. Once more, she was going to get away with it. She was no stranger to holding her nerve when things got tough. Her primal brain thrived on danger, on the thrill of the fight when peril loomed.

The storm hit her the moment she stepped outside. Venice was quaking on its foundations. The elements had been unleashed, a frenzy of wind, rain and orange dust clouds throwing everything into flux. From the south, dull crashes shook the air like the dire approach of a monster from a disaster film. A *kaiju* preparing to uproot the city.

Angélique took a few footsteps through the driving rain. There wasn't a soul around. The Aquarama was back in place, moored to the landing stage and tossing wildly on the waters of the Grand Canal. She wasn't sure if she'd be able to steer it, but it was a risk she had to take. *No – an opportunity to seize.* She pushed on towards the boat, defying the barrage of salty gusts that met her.

The landing stage was swamped in mist. Angélique could barely see ten feet in front of her, but she had the nagging sense that an unseen presence was lurking. Someone was there! The guy she'd stabbed and left for dead? The Sabatini family bodyguard? She jerked to look behind her. The coloured façade of the Veziano palace had vanished under a soupy mass of fog.

'Another chance . . .'

A plaintive cry had broken through the night. Or was it just her mind playing tricks on her?

'Why didn't you give me another chance?' the voice implored, more forcefully this time.

Angélique spun around. From the treacly haze, a figure emerged. A male form swathed in a khaki K-Way raincoat. At first she didn't register who he was, the flimsy nylon hood obscuring his hairline and rain-spattered glasses. Then she recognised him in stupefaction.

Corentin . . . Corentin Lelièvre . . .

The journalist stood over her, quivering, in all his mediocrity. In his tremoring hands, he gripped a gondola oar. A long, solid piece of wood with a flat, red-and-white striped blade that looked like a giant cake slice.

The guy was slippery. She'd known it the moment their eyes had crossed in the bar that rainy August evening. But even with the weapon he was holding, he didn't scare her. To the last, she thought she'd be able to reason with him, bring the pathetic creature to his senses. But as she opened her mouth to coax him, he rammed his oar down on her with manic force.

Angélique staggered, convinced she could still escape, but a second strike catapulted her into the waters of the Grand Canal.

And she sank into the shadowy abyss.

IV

FRAGMENTS

Historic tidal surge devastates Venice

31 December 2021
Agenzia Nazionale Stampa Associata

Venice is counting the damage after being hit by an exceptionally high tide of 191cm yesterday. Compounded by violent sirocco winds, the *acqua alta* saw waves sweep far beyond St Mark's Square and the surrounding low-lying areas, with more than three quarters of the city reported to have been affected. The surge is the second highest ever recorded in the floating city, after the all-time peak of 194cm witnessed on 4 November 1966.

The weather event has caused extensive damage, provoking major transport disruption and plunging residents and businesses into chaos. The swollen waters devastated café and restaurant terraces and inundated hotels along the Grand Canal, while the crypt and vestibule of St Mark's Basilica were also flooded. Firefighters attended to more than 300 incidents after blazes broke out across the city, although fortunately all were brought under control before the flames could spread.

Venice has been left mourning at least three deaths. In the Dorsoduro, a forty-four-year-old baker was fatally electrocuted while trying to use a sump pump to evacuate water from his bakery. The second fatality came on the island of Pellestrina, where a care home was flooded after a wave of mud swept in through the ground-floor entrance. Some twenty residents were rescued by staff, but an eighty-three-year-old woman perished in the floodwaters. Finally, a pregnant Frenchwoman, Angélique Charvet, an employee of the AcquaAlta Foundation, was found dead near the Veziano palace following an accident whose circumstances remain unclear.

The estimated cost of the damage is eye-watering – believed to be in the hundreds of millions of euros – prompting the President of the city council to declare a natural-disaster-induced state of emergency.

Although water levels had fallen by this morning, hundreds of boats and gondolas were still floating without oars in the lagoon and canals. While the storm appears to have peaked for now, the Venice tide-forecasting centre has warned that further surges can't be ruled out in the coming days.

Among Venetian residents, there is a growing mood of anger. While tidal surges are not uncommon in the city, such incidents are increasing in frequency and intensity under the effects of climate change. For twenty years, plans have been afoot to build a floating flood barrier to protect Venice from rising water levels, which should soon become operational. It has never been so keenly awaited.

AFTER THE STORM

Friday, 31 December
Santi Giovanni e Paolo Hospital
Venice

It was now hours since the storm had blown over. The wind had dropped, and a gentle winter sun had settled over the lagoon. From the colour of the sky alone, it was hard to imagine the calamity that had just ravaged the city. Below the hospital windows, however, the streets thrummed with the sound of residents, shopkeepers and restaurant owners hurrying to dry out and repair everything that was still salvageable. The water was ebbing, but only slowly. The city's wounds would take a long time to heal, and the future looked fraught. The only winners were the wellie sellers cashing in on the turmoil to lure idling tourists, who gaily donned their smiles and shared their inanely hashtagged snaps on social media.

Hooked to a drip, with his collar bone and lower abdomen in bandages, Mathias Taillefer opened his eyes without really knowing where he was. Somewhere in limbo, he deduced, hovering between heaven and earth while his fate was decided. To hand it to purgatory, the place didn't look half-bad. Golden sunlight was streaming into the room, and there was a blonde angel by his bedside.

His breathing was laboured, as if the air couldn't quite get through. His eyes met with Louise's. Dimpled chin, sparkling gaze, keen pupils; the spirited glow of her personality. It had all started in a Parisian hospital five days earlier, and it was all ending today in a Venetian hospital. His lips parted in an attempt to speak.

'You really did . . . stitch me up.'

She leant in closer. He tried to raise his voice.

'Of course you weren't there by accident, that afternoon at the Pompidou. You knew who I was from the start . . .'

Louise nodded.

'It was my biological grandmother, Margharita Bakker, who told me the truth. When I went to see her in Rotterdam last year.'

'Alice never said that she was having my baby,' Taillefer insisted.

'I know,' Louise replied.

'I haven't heard a word from her since 2003.'

'She died a few years ago. I'll explain everything.'

Taillefer touched his hand to his heart.

'I don't think I'll make it this time.'

'Stop moaning,' Louise shrugged back. 'You've never looked better.'

'What?!' he spluttered.

'A couple of stab wounds in the stomach, you're an old hand by now. Just water off a duck's back for you, isn't it?'

THE HONOUR COURT

Thursday, 23 December 2021

As she did every morning when she was in Venice, Bianca Sabatini was sipping her ritual coffee at Pasticceria Regazzoni. Gianluigi, the owner, always saved her the same two seats at the end of the counter. After taking up her place, she'd sink into her thoughts for an hour, mulling over the latest woes facing her family and their business.

Everyone thought Lisandro was the Godfather, the head of the family, but that was an illusion. The real boss was her. Always had been. She was the one who made all the decisions that mattered. Especially the tough ones. She called the shots in full cognisance, without wavering on the trigger.

That morning, a man in a red parka walked into the café and came to sit next to Bianca.

Henri Pheulpin, the Man in the Red Coat, had been summoned early, in regard to a case Bianca wanted to bring before the honour court. She slid towards him a file that she herself had prepared, cataloguing in minute detail the crimes of which Angélique Charvet stood accused.

'Our family has never been so grievously insulted,' Bianca spat, her tone icy.

As he glanced down at the file, Pheulpin couldn't resist flicking through the opening pages, which held the autopsy report on Marco Sabatini's exhumed body. A few phrases had been highlighted in fluorescent yellow: 'injection of calcium chloride', 'fibrillation', 'unmistakeable act of poisoning'.

'That girl shouldn't be on this earth,' Bianca continued. 'She belongs in the ninth circle of hell, with the other traitors and murderers.'

'A verdict will be reached as soon as possible,' Pheulpin assured her.

He was about to leave when Bianca tugged him back by the sleeve.

'I've another favour to ask of you.'

She pulled a second file from her bag.

'I can't stand traitors,' she began, handing the cardboard wallet to the Man in the Red Coat, 'but snitches sicken me even more.'

Pheulpin slipped off the elastic bands. The folder contained simply a name and a photograph. The portrait of a balding thirty-something with a sparse goatee, wearing a T-shirt emblazoned with an attempt at a funny slogan: 'Save our planet, it's the only one with beer!'

Journalist killed in scooter accident

2 January 2022
Le Parisien

A thirty-four-year-old journalist, Corentin Lelièvre, has died after being hit by a car while riding an e-scooter along Quai de Jemmapes, in the 10th arrondissement.

After the collision, the vehicle – a black BMW X4 that witnesses claim was driven by a man dressed in a red coat – fled the scene without stopping.

Our colleague was already dead by the time paramedics arrived.

An enquiry has been launched by the STJA, the Paris Prefecture's judicial accident processing service, to establish the exact circumstances of the incident.

Over recent months, fatal accidents involving e-scooters have multiplied in the capital. Many residents have become incensed by the antisocial use of the vehicles and by the lax stance of law enforcement officers, who appear to have abandoned efforts to enforce responsible riding. City council officials have directed the blame at the private operators of public-hire scooters, who are accused of not doing enough to regulate the speed and parking of the two-wheelers.

SYRINX

Paris
Gare du Nord
October 2003

Friday evening. The platform is thronged with passengers waiting for the Line 4 service to Porte d'Orléans.

Mathias Taillefer, a twenty-nine-year-old police officer, is heading home after his shift. He and his colleague have spent the evening checking alibis in the Barbès area of the city, in connection with a murder case involving Montreuil's Malian community. He slips in among the crowd and glances at his watch: 9.45 p.m. He hadn't realised it was so late. Yet another evening sacrificed. Taillefer has always struggled with the transition between work and normal life. He's always been slightly out of step, detached from the world around him, prone to the blues. This evening, for no reason he can explain, his sense of gloom and isolation is particularly acute.

While he waits for the train, he sits down on one of the orange plastic seats and pulls a book from his coat pocket: *Love in the Time of Cholera*, by Gabriel García Márquez. He skims a few lines, but very quickly looks up again, distracted by the incessant buzz of the metro. It's second nature to him, this constant state of vigilance, the need to make sure his surroundings are safe. He clocks the telltale signs of a pair of pickpockets, but the men are canny enough to spot him too and quickly make themselves scarce.

The train enters the station and comes to a stop. The doors open, releasing a wave of passengers. It's the night of the week when everyone is flocking out to restaurants and film showings, catching up with friends, making off for the weekend.

Mathias hesitates between two carriages. He doesn't know that the rest of his existence is being mapped out, right here and now. That he's facing one of those moments that can change the course of a life forever.

Mathias hesitates between two carriages. He doesn't know it, of course, but the one on the left holds Elias Abbes and his two cronies, multiple knife blows, years of pain, a direct track to hell. The one on the right, a perfectly ordinary future.

Left or right?

Suddenly, he catches sight of a blonde woman hurrying along the platform, dressed in a Venetian-yellow jacket and a white blouse. Slung over her shoulder is a Pearl flute case, and poking out of her tote bag is a page of sheet music. In a blur, he glimpses the title: *Syrinx* by Claude Debussy.

Their eyes cross, lock for a moment. Mathias steps after her into the carriage. The one on the left. All for a smile, for a flash of blonde in the gloom, for a waft of *Miss Dior*, for a promise of music, for a spark of intelligence in a passing gaze, for a dimpled chin.

The alarm sounds. The doors close again. The train sets off.

Deciding forever the fate of its passengers.

ALICE BAKKER

Paris
September 2009

She'd come with the sole intention of seeing her. She'd caught the late-morning train from Rotterdam and ambled through Paris until she'd neared the Jardin des Grands Explorateurs, where Louise's school was located. There, she'd waited for pick-up time slightly apart from the other 'playground mums'. She might have been the mother, but she'd never collected her daughter from school.

Alice Bakker had never felt the maternal instinct that society so prized, but on being told she had terminal cancer, Alice's first thought had been for her: Louise, her five-year-old daughter.

It was the girl's 'father', Laurent Collange, who'd come for Louise that day. The pair of them had walked to the Jardin du Luxembourg for an after-school snack. Alice had followed at a safe distance to avoid being seen. The toy sailing boat hut, the wide octagonal pond, the peals of children's laughter, the squabbling pigeons, the sea-green chairs . . . the old gardens hadn't lost their charm. But what captivated

Alice more than anything was the little girl. The way she lit up everything around her. Hard as it was to believe now, it really was Alice who'd carried her for nine months before bringing her into the world. Before her broken mind had decided to abandon her.

So perfection did exist after all, in the form of a little girl hopping between the shafts of sunlight filtering through the boughs of the horse chestnuts. Long, wavy fair hair, oval-rimmed glasses, Peter Pan collar. That fairness was Alice's own! She'd been blonde and beautiful once, before she became an emaciated, tattooed old punk with no sunshine left in her.

Despite her physical transformation, Laurent Collange had recognised her from afar. Alice had never told her ex-partner that Louise wasn't his biological daughter. Laurent must have nursed his suspicions, but he'd studiously avoided asking questions and had embraced fatherhood with every ounce of himself. Watching him now, Alice could read his panic at the thought that she'd come to take his little miracle away. But that wasn't why she was there. She wanted only to see Louise one last time. To etch that beaming face on her memory, in the hope that its light would comfort her when the time came to sink into the shadows.

A LEBANESE SPRING

Beirut
Achrafieh district
April 2022

Taillefer had arrived from Paris the previous night, on the last Middle East Airlines flight which had landed with a three-hour delay. He'd bunked down at a small hotel in the Gemmayzeh and had fallen asleep almost instantly, despite the basic bedding and oppressive heat.

It was only now, the following morning, that he'd been able to stroll through the streets of the capital. He'd first visited years earlier, in the mid-nineties, back when Beirut was the 'Switzerland of the Middle East'. At the time, he'd been seduced by the wildly romantic feel of the city, which was like no place he'd ever known.

Today, all that had changed radically. Lebanon was in turmoil, caught between multiple crises. The double explosion in Beirut's port at the height of summer 2020 had plunged the country into an unprecedented state of chaos. Life had become a daily ordeal. Securing food, electricity, petrol and healthcare were suddenly Herculean struggles. Yet despite their predicament, the people were as warm as ever. Taillefer had spent all morning chatting to friendly strangers he'd met in cafés and shops.

One o'clock. The air was warm and humid. Gathering his strength, he heaved his way up the Saint Nicolas Stairs – the longest outdoor stairway in the Middle East, comprised of 125 weather-worn steps that gave onto the Greek Orthodox Sursock quarter. The area had been badly hit by the blast, and many houses and apartment blocks still wore the scars. The cop pushed on to the sweeping public gardens around St Nicolas Orthodox Church, then settled on a bench near a large fountain to wait. It was here, he'd discovered, that Lena brought her lunch in nice weather. The vet's surgery where she worked was a stone's throw away, on Charles Malek Avenue.

He could feel his heart quickening. A heart that wasn't entirely his own. Despite having rehearsed the scene countless times in his mind, he was shaking like a leaf. Over recent months, thanks to Louise, he'd slowly begun to turn a corner. He'd recovered some of his old energy, clawed back a little faith in life, had even allowed himself to look to the future. It was Louise who'd convinced him that the trip was worth making, that he needed to have it out with Lena. He'd stalled before taking the plunge. Even now, he was racked with doubt, but he knew he couldn't put it off any longer. He had to capitalise on his modest progress. Life was too unpredictable, capable of sending everything you'd built tumbling down overnight.

He'd been on his bench for ten minutes when Lena's outline appeared behind the jets of the fountain. Taillefer stood up, took a gulp of courage, and clung to what he knew best: walking into the firing line with a brave face, ready to weather whatever storm came his way.

He thought of Stella Petrenko, who'd shared that same defiant spirit, that same ability to stagger back up even after being wounded, disfigured, left for dead. He thought of Angélique Charvet, who'd believed she could master her fate and make her own luck. He thought of Louise, a blast from a past that he'd never known existed, an unexpected gift from life who'd saved him from the jaws of hell. The image of his daughter soothed him and gave him hope. And letting his heart do the talking, he went to speak to Lena.

MONTPARNASSE CEMETERY

Paris

8 October 2022

As he now did every day, Mathias had risen early. The house was still sleeping, but the lull would end in a few minutes' time. Two whirlwinds, nine-year-old Baptiste and seven-year-old Anna, would soon tear out of bed and sweep through the building with their Panini albums, Lego bricks and Harry Potter figurines.

In the kitchen, Mathias was already in full swing: butter, thick honey, jam, slices of bread ready for toasting, fresh orange juice that he squeezed directly with his bearlike hands.

Lessons began at eight-thirty. Each morning he deposited the tearaways at school, a twenty-five-minute walk from the house to Boulevard Edgar Quinet, then repeated the journey in reverse every afternoon.

At last, he felt like he'd found his place. That he was part of a whole that went beyond himself. Living with Lena and her children had given his life purpose. A positive grounding that he'd always craved. Piecing back together his splintered heart had been a bit like kintsugi, the ancient Japanese art of repairing pottery with powdered gold. His scars remained visible not as trophies, not as gung-ho assertions that 'whatever doesn't kill me makes me stronger', but simply as marks of acceptance. The blows he'd suffered had tested him, but they hadn't broken him to the point of erasing all hope for the future.

After dropping the children at school, he often headed home through Montparnasse Cemetery, to amble among the graves. Over the course of his visits, he'd come to enjoy the company of the dead. He liked stopping to chat to them, and their conversations did him good.

Simon Verger, the man whose heart he carried, wasn't buried there. His grave was somewhere in the Loire-Atlantique. It made no odds. Mathias didn't need that kind of proximity, not when he lived with Simon's heart in his chest. Almost every day, he gave him news of the children and Lena, telling him about their new life in Paris, keen to make him understand that he hadn't taken his place, that he was simply watching over them. And that if, one day, something should threaten their family, he'd stand ready to protect them. He'd throw his body in the way of punches, knife blades, missiles, bullets. That was one thing he knew how to do.

Mathias Taillefer didn't believe in God, but he liked to think that maybe, somewhere up there, Simon Verger could see all that and was grateful to him.

AUTHOR'S NOTE

For dramatic effect, some allusions – such as to the Big Wheel in the Jardin des Tuileries (Chapter 4), the sculpture by Christo and Jeanne-Claude (Chapter 12) and the MOSE project in Venice (Part IV) – have been adapted slightly to fit the time frame of the novel.